FOREIGN EXCHANGE

FOREIGN EXCHANGE

A Novel By

Jimmy Sangster

W · W · NORTON & COMPANY · INC · *New York*

To : Mon

FOREIGN EXCHANGE

CHAPTER ONE

SOMETIME BACK I read an article which said that London was the most swinging city in the world. I don't think the man who wrote the article had ever been to London or, if he had, he hadn't been to my part of it. My part doesn't swing, it just hangs there. I also read that London was timeless. If, by timeless, the writer meant that everything stays the same uniform shade of grey, then I can go along with him. Grey people in grey buildings, living grey little lives. And the greyest life of them all is mine.

It had been a long, hard winter. Expenses had been running at their customary level of stupidity, with income limping along in the rear falling further and further behind. And now it was Monday. It's a rotten stinking day is Monday. And just lately I've started to believe that every day is Monday, even Friday. Everyone who could had spent the weekend away from London, leaving it to the grey people. Being a founder member, I had stayed with them.

Mary, the only light in the murk of my existence, had recently taken up horse riding. She would disappear each weekend into the country, there to exercise her urges on the back of a horse. She had started by asking me to come along with her. If she could learn to ride, then so could I, was her attitude. But after making a number of fatuous excuses I was finally forced to admit that while horses for betting on are fair enough, horses for riding on scare the living daylights out of me. Their superior bloody attitude intimidates me, and the distance from the ground one is required to perch is, to my way of thinking, suicidal. So our long weekends doing nothing except each other had come to an abrupt end. Booted and spurred, she would drive away on a Saturday morning and return, sore and satisfied, late on Sunday night. I was too pig-headed to want to hear about her equine prowess, or how the nineteen-year-old riding instructor had developed a serious crush on her. So I left her alone on Sunday evenings, and gradually my weekends deteriorated into a slough of boredom. This one had been no exception.

Saturday had been shopping in the morning and 'Grandstand' on the box in the afternoon. About six I had thought for a moment about taking myself out to dinner. Then I had decided that I couldn't be bothered. I had ended up with bacon and eggs and more television.

Sunday had been Sunday papers and a lunchtime drink in a Chelsea pub. At this pub, the thing to do was to drink cider and sit on the pavement. I drank brown ale, sitting on a bar stool with my elbows in a pool of stale beer. A hundred years ago I had sat on the pavement to drink my cider, but now cider gave me a headache and the pavement aggravated my piles.

Sunday afternoon had been television again, and Sunday evening another pub. This pub was supposed to be chic, but there weren't any chic people in London, and to me it was just another pub where beer was twopence a pint dearer to help pay for the regency striped curtains.

*   *   *

That had been my weekend in the swingingest city in the world and now, rejuvenated by all that excitement, I joined the commuters on the way to the office.

My office lies between a coffee bar and a strip joint just off Old Compton Street. This is in Soho, the 'wicked' section of the Swinging City. To a fourteen-year-old it may be wicked. To me it's just plain nasty.

Sometime over the weekend some joker had peed through the letter box all over the entrance hall. But this was a common occurrence and I didn't even notice the smell any more. Occasionally I'd indulge in flights of fancy that ran to setting some sort of jaw toothed trap inside the letter box. But, with my luck, if I'd hooked anything I would have been arrested for causing grievous bodily harm.

I avoided the fourth stair, which could break the leg of the unwary, and opened the outer door of my office. Miss Roberts was already there, rattling the teacups. She smiled at me as I came in.

'Good morning, Mr Smith,' she said. 'Did you have a nice weekend?'

I told her that I had spent a quiet weekend.

'We went to the coast,' she said brightly.

Miss Roberts had been working for me for three years, and I had never asked her who 'we' included. It couldn't have been a boy friend. If it wasn't for the fact that she wore a skirt and used the 'Ladies' on the third floor, I would have taken money that she was a fellow. She had a trim little moustache and her voice could best be described as a full-toned baritone. But under this formidable exterior lurked an excited young girl of motherly inclinations. She was kind to the point of embarrassment, and she looked after Stubbs and me like a protective hen. Stubbs shared the offices with me. We each used the outer office and the services of Miss Roberts, and we each had our own room leading off it. While I ran a sometime private investigation business, Stubbs ran a sometime theatrical agency. Occasionally this would cause the outer office to be graced with expectant young female hopefuls who had somehow been recommended to Stubbs as a man who could further their artistic careers. If he did further their careers, it must have been straight into the arms of another agent, as I never saw the same girl twice.

As for Stubbs himself, I saw little of him. Three or four weeks could go by without us bumping into each other. On the odd occasions when we did meet, the encounters were overlaid with a subtle form of embarrassment, due to us both knowing everything about each other, courtesy of Miss Roberts. If I knew that he hadn't paid his share of Miss Roberts' salary for two weeks, I also knew that he knew that I'd been served with a writ for non-payment of my car instalments. We were both dead losses at our chosen professions, and we both knew that the other was aware of it. The sensible thing to have done would have been to slap him on the back and ask him out for a beer. That way we could have cried in it together and to hell with the embarrassment. But I never did, and neither did he. So we went our separate ways, tied together by Miss Roberts and our common failure to scratch a decent living.

All this made it quite a surprise when Miss Roberts followed me into my office, clutching the first of an endless supply of cups of tea.

'Mr Stubbs would like to see you,' she said.

My first thought was that he wanted to borrow money.

Then I remembered that he knew me as well as I knew him, and he would have been aware of the futility of such an idea.

'Is he here now?' I asked.

'Yes, and he'd like to see you just as soon as you can spare him a moment.'

'Wheel him in then,' I said. He was the one requesting the interview, so let him come to me. While Miss Roberts went to fetch him, I took off my coat and hung it up. There was no mail, so I took a couple of old reports from my drawer and spread them around on top of my desk. If he was going to ask for my time, as opposed to money, I wanted to create the impression that it was valuable.

There was a tap on the door and in he came. He's a small, birdlike man, with neat precise movements. But this morning it was different; his movements were sluggish and his feathers bedraggled.

'Good of you to spare me a moment, John,' he said.

So he did want something from me. He'd never called me anything but Mr Smith before.

'Sit down Harvey,' I said. I, too, could use Christian names. He sat and plucked nervously at his trouser crease for a moment. He was on a hook and, being ignorant, I couldn't help him off. I waited.

'How's business?' he asked finally.

'Just fine, Harvey,' I said. 'You?'

'Good,' he said. 'Very good.'

Having lied our way through the overture, he opened the first movement.

'There's a girl,' he said. And there he stopped.

There was nothing I could say, so I just sat and tried to look interested and intelligent at the same time. The former wasn't difficult, I *was* interested. I'd long had Stubbs tagged as a fairy. As for looking intelligent, I've been told that if I frown a little and can manage a slight squint, the effect is passable.

He coughed twice, cleared his throat, and twitched in his chair.

'There's a girl,' he said again. I gave him all the help I could. 'Yes, Harvey?'

'There's a girl,' he said for the third time. But from there on in he needed no help. Once he stepped over the edge, there was no stopping him.

'She came to see me four months ago. Perhaps you saw her in the office? Pretty little thing with blonde hair, blue eyes and big knockers.' They all had blonde hair, blue eyes and big knockers, but I kept my mouth shut.

'Not much talent, but quite a nice singing voice and beautifully built. I took her on to my books. I liked the kid as a matter of fact. I told her she weren't no Marilyn Monroe, likewise she weren't no Barbra Streisand. But I said that, handled properly, she could no doubt earn herself a fair to middling share of scratch on the number two type circuits. She didn't seem to mind. Seems she knew about the Monroe-Streisand bit, and all she wanted was a small forty pound a week job, and to hell with her name in neon.'

Right then I could have done with a small forty pound a week job myself, but Stubbs was in full flow now and I didn't interrupt.

'So I booked her for a one-nighter down a pub in the City. Sort of dummy run. She went down fine and I fixed her three or four more dates on the same circuit. She weren't earning no forty a week, but then she weren't on Assistance either. I took to visiting the places she played. The neighbourhood's a bit

14

crumbum, and so I'd take her back to her pad after she'd done her show.'

There was a pause. I jumped in.

'And?' I said.

'And nothing,' he said. 'Never set foot inside the front door.'

'But she's pregnant and she wants you to pay for the operation,' I suggested.

Stubbs looked at me wide-eyed. If I'd just promulgated the theory of relativity, I couldn't have impressed him more.

'How did you know?' he asked.

'I guessed,' I said. 'You don't think she's pregnant?'

'She could have fifteen buns in the oven for all I know,' he said. 'But one thing's for sure – I'm not the baker.'

'What does she say when you tell her that?'

'Nothing,' he said. 'She says nothing at all. She just smiles at me in a special way.'

'Special how?'

'Like one of those adverts for insurance where the bird's looking at her husband who's just taken out a bloody great policy. Like "Drop dead, but don't make too much noise about it".'

I knew the look well.

'What do you want me to do Harvey?' I said.

'Go and see her. Tell her it's Harvey Stubbs she's got her hooks into, not Lew and Leslie Grade. Ten per cent of what my clients earn doesn't add up to two hundred guinea abortions.'

'Is that what she's asking?'

'She tells me she's got the quack all picked out,' he said.

'For two hundred guineas, he's no quack.'

'He is if he manages to get *my* baby out of that cheap hooker.'

'Have you tried telling her to go jump in the lake?'

'Sure I told her,' said Stubbs. 'She just smiles that smile some more and says she'll sick the law on to me.'

'There's no law against poking,' I said.

'There is when you poke a fifteen-year-old,' he said.

He continued fast, before I could comment. 'So help me, she looks twenty-two,' he said. 'And I didn't anyway.'

'She's got quite a case,' I said.

'Then why doesn't she lay it before the guy who packed it?'

'Perhaps she has,' I said.

He thought about this for a moment. Then his eyes widened. 'Clip us both,' he said.

'Why just the two of you? If she'd like to spread her net a bit, there's no limit to the number of suckers she can con.'

'There is as far as I'm concerned,' he said. 'I don't have no two hundred guineas, and if I did I wouldn't hand it over to her.'

'What would you hand over?' I said.

'You mean to make a deal?'

I nodded.

'With that cheap whore,' he said. 'Why should I let her screw me?'

'She already has. We've got to make sure the screw isn't too tight.'

He thought about this for a moment; then he came up with an alternative.

'You wouldn't like to lean on her a little, would you?'

My leaning days were long gone. Not since I quit the Service had I leaned on anybody. At least, not physically. I told him so.

'How big a deal?' he said finally.

'How much can you afford?'

'Nothing,' he said. 'But I could scrape up twenty-five at a pinch.'

Even I could have managed twenty-five. Business must have been worse than I thought.

'I'll put it to her,' I said.

'How will you put it?'

'I'll tell her if she lets you off the hook she can have twenty-five guineas.'

'Pounds,' he said.

I ignored the interruption. 'If she doesn't want to accept it, you'll fight.'

'You bet,' he said. 'I'll have her teeth knocked down her throat.'

'I didn't mean fight fight. I meant legal fight.'

'Oh,' he said. I thought he looked disappointed. He had a nasty streak in him, I decided. Funny I hadn't noticed it before.

'Let's have her name and address and I'll go see her,' I said.

He hesitated for a moment. 'About your fee?'

I decided to be magnanimous, mainly because, whatever fee I named, I wouldn't be getting it.

'No fee,' I said. 'Perhaps you can do me a favour one day.'

I was going to be pretty hard pressed on the day I needed a favour from Harvey Stubbs, but it never hurt to make a person beholden to you, especially if that person shared the same office. Maybe one week I wouldn't be able to find my half of the rent. Then I could remind him of how big I'd been. Apart from that I was quite interested in taking a look at the girl who had managed to con a sharp operator like Stubbs with one of the oldest tricks in the book.

'Her name is Anne,' he said. 'Anne Ballard. Flat 625, Chelsea Park Towers.'

It figured. I knew the block of flats well. It was known in the trade as The Rabbit Warren. There were ten floors with fifty one-room apartments on each floor. You can't really *live* in a one room apartment, but you can do just about everything else. And that pretty well covered it as far as The Rabbit Warren was concerned.

I brushed aside Stubbs' effusive thanks, telling him to save them until I was able to do some good. He parted with a twenty-five guinea cheque like a man parting with his eye teeth, but I promised to let him have it back if I wasn't successful. He seemed to forget the fact that if I wasn't able to make her take it, he was liable to be lumbered with one for eight times the amount. But I knew how he felt as he watched me fold the cheque and put it in my notecase.

He thanked me again, and again I reminded him not to be premature. As he left the office, his movements were neat and precise, and he was birdlike once more. As far as he was concerned, the ball had been passed out of his court, even if only temporarily. I hoped for his sake he hadn't misplaced his trust. At least I had discovered he'd got balls, which was something I hadn't known before. And having made the discovery, I found myself almost liking him.

I didn't believe for one second that he hadn't poked the girl. People just aren't like that. If a girl sleeps around, people oblige her, especially people like Harvey Stubbs. Anyway, even the sloppiest con artist isn't going to try to palm the offspring on to a fellow who hasn't even been there.

*   *   *

I hadn't visited The Rabbit Warren since a small affair I'd had going for me about five years ago. It hadn't changed. The porters still studiously ignored everyone who came in or out, minding nobody's business but their own. The tenants preferred it that way. I rode one of the elevators up to the sixth, and then walked down what seemed like half a mile of dark corridor until I located 625. I rang the front door bell and, for good measure, I knocked as well.

A girl answered the door and right about there I started to think there was something seriously wrong with Harvey Stubbs. She didn't look twenty-two, she didn't even look fifteen. She was about ten.

'Yes?' she said primly.

'Miss Ballard, please,' I said.

'She's gone to the shops. Would you like to wait?'

She stood back, holding the door open for me and, although I should have known better, I walked in. The apartment was neat and clean. There were two divans, both made up as settees, and the sort of anonymous furniture one finds in multi-apartment blocks.

'Would you like to sit down?' she said.

I sat down and the child stood four feet away from me and regarded me solemnly for what seemed like six long months.

'Anne usually asks gentlemen callers if they'd like a drink. Would you like a drink?'

'Very much,' I said. She smiled and trotted off through the door which I knew from memory led to the tiny kitchen. Some people have the happy knack of being able to communicate with children. I even have trouble communicating with my own age group, and anyone below the age of twenty might as well be from a different species, so vast is our lack of communication.

A couple of minutes later the little charmer reappeared carrying a glass full of what I took to be gin or vodka, but in fact turned out to be water.

I sipped it and made appreciative noises. Then I decided that, as I was supposed to be working, I might as well work.

'Does your mother have many gentlemen callers?' I said, feeling like a bastard.

'I don't know,' she said. 'She lives in Barnsley.'

'Miss Ballard is your . . .?' I let the question hang.

'Anne's my sister,' she said. 'I've lived with her ever since Mum ran off with the telly man and Dad went inside for doing him over.'

As a potted family biography, it seemed to cover all the salient facts. I sipped my water again and tried to think of something amusing to say.

'It's been a nice day,' I managed finally.

'Very nice,' she said.

'It was terrible yesterday,' I sparkled.

'Awful,' she agreed.

And there the conversation ground to a halt, where it remained for five minutes until Anne Ballard arrived.

She came in behind a parcel of groceries which hid her face from me. So I looked at the rest of her, as she headed straight for the kitchen without being aware she had a gentleman caller. It was no hardship at all, and I started to hope that her face wouldn't let the rest of her down. She swore fluently in the kitchen as she dropped something on her foot, and her little sister didn't bat an eyelid. Then she came out of the kitchen and saw me sitting there clutching my glass of water.

'Hi!' she said.

'Miss Ballard?'

'That's why you're here, isn't it?'

She had wide blue eyes, a small nose and a mouth that looked good enough to make you want to be eaten.

'I gave him a drink,' said the little girl.

'So I see,' she said, looking at my glass. 'Tell me what you want and I may offer you another.'

'My name is Smith. John Smith,' I started.

She grinned, showing perfect teeth.

'I'd hate to be with you when you're signing a hotel register,' she said. 'And you can have that drink, whatever you want.'

She took my glass and disappeared into the kitchen again. My main thought about now was that if Stubbs hadn't slept with her, he must be queer after all; and if he had, he was a dirty rotten bastard. If this girl was the sleeping around kind, there must have been a queue from here to Piccadilly Circus every night. And I knew who was going to be first in line next time. But even while leching in my mind, other wheels were clicking. She couldn't be just fifteen, that was for sure. And I'd just about decided that Stubbs had got the whole thing screwed up, or we were dealing with two different people, when she came back with my drink. This one looked like water, too, but it was vodka. And it was on the rocks, the way I like it. If it had been possible, she would have gone up a couple more notches in my estimation, but there wasn't room. She may have been no Barbra Streisand or Marilyn Monroe, but she didn't need to be from where I was sitting.

'I suppose Harvey sent you,' she said, dragging me back to earth with a jerk.

'He didn't send me,' I said. 'I came of my own free will.'

'Harvey Stubbs nevertheless?' she said.

'Nevertheless.'

'I saw your name on the door the day I went to see Harvey,' she said by way of explanation. 'Darling, slip downstairs and get me some cigarettes from the machine.'

She handed her sister some money and the little girl left dutifully. Then she sat down in the armchair opposite me and crossed her legs neatly and elegantly. They were good legs, very good.

'It's your move,' she said.

I lifted my eyes and cleared my throat.

'Harvey thinks you may have got a mistaken impression as to his earning capacity,' I said. 'He is quite incapable of finding the sum you mentioned.'

She didn't bat an eyelid. 'Tell him if he leaves me alone, he's off the hook.'

I didn't say anything. There didn't seem to be anything to say.

'Surprise surprise,' she said finally. 'The whore has got a heart of gold.'

Now that I'd done what I came for, I couldn't think of any excuse for staying around, so I made movements preparatory to getting to my feet.

'Aren't you intrigued?' she said.

I nodded. 'Very.'

'Shall I tell you something?'

If it meant I could stay a little longer she could have told me anything. And I *was* intrigued. I subsided again, regretting that I'd downed the last of my drink. She must have been a thought-reader. 'I'll get you another drink,' she said, and took my glass and disappeared into the kitchen again. I looked around the flat from where I was sitting. It was neat and tidy, and somehow the anonymity of the furniture was dispelled by the small personal possessions that lay around. There were a couple of large teddy bears, one on each bed, and a few snapshots of the two of them on holiday. One snap was tucked in the corner of a picture frame holding the photograph of a weak chinned man about forty-five. If this was Dad, I couldn't see him doing over a disinterested boy scout, let alone an amorously inclined telly man.

She returned with my fresh drink and sat down again.

'Are you married?' she said.

I shook my head. 'I was. But not any longer.'

'What do you do for sex?'

'The same as everyone else,' I said. 'I'm normal.'

'I don't mean that. I mean, do you chase nineteen year old girls?'

'I'm too old,' I lied.

'That makes you about the only man in London who is. This flat is a bloody citadel, where I defend my honour nightly. A man walks me to the front door – and let battle commence. I've talked to them, argued with them, wrestled with them. I've even banged one on the head with a bottle. Because I sing in a couple of clubs and live alone, I'm supposed to be easy meat. I'm not knocking sex, I like it. But it's got to be on my terms and when I want it. I'm sick of everything in trousers between the ages of seventeen and seventy behaving like a stag in rut just because I'm polite and don't bang them in the mouth when they start to leer.'

'You're not pregnant?' I asked.

'I'm not that stupid,' she said. 'Neither am I fifteen years old.'

I grinned, trying to make it look avuncular and not like a leer.

'I didn't think you were.'

'But it works,' she said. 'Tell a man you're only fifteen and you need a two hundred guinea abortion and it's amazing how quickly his blood pressure goes down.'

'Harvey Stubbs was persistent?'

'Harvey Stubbs was a bastard,' she said. 'He was the one I had to use the bottle on.'

'Bully for Harvey,' I said.

There was a pause.

'Satisfied?' she said finally.

I took that as a signal that I'd outstayed my time. I swallowed my drink and clambered to my feet.

'I'll tell Harvey if he lays off he's got nothing to worry about.'

She stood up. 'But I don't want to see him around here again,' she said.

'You won't,' I said. Then I suddenly remembered the cheque. I fished it out of my pocket and showed it to her.

'Want it?'

She shook her head. 'He probably needs it more than I do.'

She followed me to the door. Just before she opened it she looked at me steadily for a beat.

'What *do* you do for sex?' she asked.

'I get by.'

'You're not every girl's dream of home,' she said. 'But I imagined you did. Come and hear me sing one night.'

'Where?'

'Ask Harvey. He's still my agent, even if he is a bastard.'

She opened the door and I nearly collided with kid sister, who was just coming in. The little girl smiled brightly at me as she slipped past me into the flat.

'Apart from anything else,' said Anne. 'This is a one-roomed flat.'

'Yes,' I said.

She closed the door quietly behind me and I retraced my way along the corridors back to earth.

*　　*　　*

'I met some competition today,' I said. Mary looked up from her scrambled eggs.

'Competition for whom?'

'You.'

'You're frightening me to death,' she said, as she resumed eating.

Mary is the lovely, leggy blonde with whom I have my arrangement. It's not much of an arrangement; I'm in love with her, I think. She feels sorry for me, I believe. She has the casual elegance of the model, combined with a devastating charm that has been known to stun the most hardened buyers. But underneath her professional shell she is as soft as marshmallow, the gentlest, warmest thing I've ever snuggled up to.

'You're not the only fish in the sea,' I said.

'I am in yours,' she said, not even looking up. 'No other fish would put up with you.'

'I was led to believe that if I cared to make an advance, it would not be unkindly received,' I said.

'You were conned.'

She shovelled up her last mouthful of scrambled egg and,

getting to her feet, she headed for the kitchen. She limped heavily due to an altercation she had had with her horse that weekend.

'Your leg's going to be black tomorrow,' I said.

'So's your eye if you don't stop throwing up your girl friends in my face.'

This was the first time she had ever intimated that there might be a shade of jealousy in her and I felt unreasonably pleased. Like the idiot I often am, I pursued the idea.

'I'll bet she doesn't waste her weekends climbing all over horses and nearly breaking her leg.'

Mary rattled a couple of dishes in the sink. 'I bet she doesn't waste her evenings feeding a *schnorrer* like you.' Being in the rag trade her speech could at times lapse into the Jewish vernacular, especially when she was feeling angry. And I still didn't leave it alone.

'At least now I might have someone with whom to spend those long, wet weekends.

Mary suddenly appeared in the arch that led to the kitchen. 'You spend one long wet minute with her and you can go somewhere else to get laid.'

'I don't come here to get laid.'

'So you keep telling me, but you give a pretty good imitation of it three nights a week.'

I realised I had long overstepped the mark, so I tried some back pedalling. 'I'm joking,' I said, trying to look contrite.

'You're not,' she said. 'You're trying to needle me. And you're making a bloody good job of it.'

'Are you needled?'

'Yes I am,' she said, and flounced back into the kitchen.

I gathered up a couple of plates and followed her in.

'I'm sorry,' I said, trying to nuzzle the back of her neck. She brought her head back sharply, catching me on the bridge of the nose.

'Ouch!' I yelled.

'Serve you right,' she said. 'You're a sadist.'

'You don't bash a sadist,' I said. 'You allow him to bash you.'

My eyes were watering, but I made more of it than was necessary, and her face started to soften into the gentle expression I loved.

'Did I hurt you?' she asked.

'Yes you did.'

She put her arms around my neck and kissed me on the nose. 'There,' she said. 'All better.'

Then she pulled back a little and looked at me with her wide, grey eyes. '*Did* you meet a girl today?'

'As a matter of fact I did. Professionally of course.'

'Yours or hers?'

'Mine. I thought she was a con artist. Turned out she wasn't.'

'What was she?'

'Just a girl alone in the big city trying to protect her virtue.'

'I can feel for her,' said Mary. 'It's not easy.' She walked back into the living-room and started to unzip her dress.

'I'm not complaining,' I said. 'But isn't it a little early for bed.' It was seven thirty.

'I've got a date,' she said, stepping out of her dress.

I watched her walk over to one of the wall cupboards and fish around for another dress. 'Have we got time to . . .?'

She didn't even let me finish. 'No. He'll be here in half an hour.'

I felt like reminding her that the day I could last half an hour, someone should give me a medal. But she was way ahead of me. 'It'll take me twenty minutes to put a face on, and you know how terrible I look after we've made love.'

I thought she looked marvellous after we'd made love. She looked warm and soft and defenceless. But obviously tonight's date didn't require her to look warm or soft, so I started looking round for my shoes which I'd taken off as soon as I had arrived.

I didn't ask her who her date was with. I never did. As long as I wasn't prepared to offer her any more in our relationship than I did already, I was in no position to pry into what she did when she wasn't with me. It was a pretty unsatisfactory arrangement, but it was the best I could manage. Besides, while our affair was kept on the casual side, I wasn't forcing her into making any decision about me which could have backfired and blown up in my face. Because whichever way you sliced it, I was no gift. I was pushing forty (not too hard) and I was constantly on my uppers. I was losing my hair and fighting a constant battle against overweight. My sexual prowess ranged wildly between the indifferent and the downright bad. So why put this lovely creature in a position where she was going to have to decide that I was all, or nothing at all? I wanted to, but I was scared of the way she would decide.

I found my shoes and jammed my feet into them. I could see her reflection in the mirror on the wall as she rummaged through the wardrobe. Brown flesh and white lace, and I felt myself weakening fast. So I got out of the place before discretion really took a belting and I asked her to marry me.

28

She called me back when I was half way down the stairs. She was standing at the door to her apartment, having slipped on a housecoat.

'I'll be home by eleven,' she said.

'Not a very heavy date?'

'You're my only heavy date,' she said. 'Idiot that I am.'

She kissed me and shut the door in my face.

*   *   *

On my way home I bought an evening paper. There was the usual crisis on the front page along with a picture of the Prime Minister gazing blandly from a two column photograph. He'd just made a speech in which he had said that we must all put our shoulders to the wheel, increase our productivity and cut down on our spending. If I cut down any on my spending I'd starve to death. Beneath the photograph, which was as inspiring as a plate of cold custard, was another story about how fifteen hundred car workers were out on strike because one of their number had said 'fuck' to the foreman and been given the sack.

The Antonov story was on page four. Gregori Antonov had been sentenced to fifteen years. About bloody time too, I thought. I'd been out of the Service for five years, and I'd been working on the case a year before that. Gregori Antonov, sometime Ukranian, sometime Albanian, sometime any other nationality that took his fancy; a forty-five year old agent-cum-con-artist *par excellence*. He had arrived in this country ten years ago and armed with unlimited funds and a black-mailing turn of mind, had proceeded to screw or buy classified information from any or everybody who could lay the remotest claim to know anything of value. It took the Service four years

29

to realise he was at work, and then, it seems, another six to do anything about it.

I read the story casually at first. Then I read it again. Nobody knew better than I did that the Service was capable of making a balls-up. Indeed, when I had been working for them five years ago, I'd been personally involved in, and sometimes responsible for, some monumental cock-ups. It was one of these hideous miscalculations that had caused me to pack it all in. Even today, with five years of comparative poverty behind me, I'd still break out in a cold sweat at some of the things I'd done in the cause of patriotism and sixteen hundred pounds a year. So I had no illusions about the Service. But six years to pin down one man seemed to be going it a bit, even for Max.

Dear Max! I'd managed not to think about him for nearly six months now, and was becoming pleasantly accustomed to the happy state. I hadn't clapped eyes on him since he had conned me into a triple cross involving a book of names, a Chinese Albanian by the name of Berat and a particularly murky shooting match in the wilds of Kent.* After that I had been forced to hand him back a considerable sum of money in exchange for my release from a mental institution into which he'd had me thrown complete with certificate of insanity.

Perhaps he was no longer at the helm. Perhaps he'd met with a fatal accident. I rolled these thoughts around in my mind luxuriously for a moment. Then I thought: 'What the hell?' Somebody had to do the incredibly dirty work that went on just below the surface and, if you're going to work with mud, it's as well that you've got a muddy mind. Max was right for the job, his mind was like the bottom of a bog.

I put the Antonov story out of my mind. I donned my best

* See 'private i'

blue worsted and a pint of after-shave, and drove down through the City to the pub where Anne Ballard was singing that night.

*　　*　　*

The place was really jumping. It took me three minutes to locate the bar through the smoke haze, and another five to elbow my way through to it. The noise was catastrophic; a mixture of laughter, shouting, chatter and yelling. I don't go much on the East End. It depresses me more than it should, but you have to hand it to them; when it comes to enjoying themselves they have no equal. I contrasted this place with some of my local pubs, usually decorated by pasty faced boys or girls – one couldn't be sure – who only raised their nasal voices above a whisper to insult the barman. Here, the men looked like men, and the women looked the way a woman was supposed to look – feminine. Most of the customers in the place would have put a boot in your face as soon as look at you, but they were off duty now and having a ball. If they knocked their birds about when they got home, that was their business; here in public they mostly treated them with a courtesy that unfortunately went out with Edward VII.

I screamed my order to the barmaid and, when she shoved my drink at me and gobbled up my money, I managed to get it across to her that I wanted to know what time Anne Ballard came on. She glanced at the clock behind her.

'Five minutes,' she yelled. 'After the group.'

It was only then that I realised there was a group playing. Jammed on to an undersized stage against the far wall, four young tearaways were slamming away at electric guitars and singing lustily. I assumed they were singing, because their mouths kept opening and closing. I certainly couldn't hear them. I doubt if they could even hear themselves. If Anne Ballard had to make her living singing to this lot, my heart bled for her. I started to regret that I hadn't forced her to take Stubbs' twenty-five guinea cheque. But if I couldn't hear her, at least I could see her, so I started to shove my way over towards the stage so as to be ready when she appeared.

I reached the edge of the stage just as the group bellowed their last chord. Standing with my nose practically inside the bass guitar I could hear that they *had* been singing, and I felt a little sorry for them. But they didn't seem to mind. They took four quick bows to an audience who hadn't even been aware that they had started, let alone finished. Then they scrambled down off the stage and elbowed their way towards the bar in a wedge formation.

A man got up from a chair to go to the toilet and I managed to beat an old lady to it, dragging it up close to the stage. And then, quite suddenly, all noise in the bar ceased. If a Black Maria had driven in through the doors, the effect couldn't have been bettered. I looked around to see what the excitement was all about, and there was Anne Ballard. Unfortunately she wasn't using the stage. There were some stairs leading up to a half landing on the far side of the pub, and that's where she was standing, a good fifty feet and five hundred people away from me. But even from there she looked good. She was wearing a simple little black dress and a black ribbon in her blonde hair. And that was all. No sequins, no jewelry, no trimmings. She looked about sixteen and as defenceless as a babe at a Mafia convention.

Somebody started to play the piano somewhere, and she picked up a hand mike and started to sing. I've got a tin ear myself; to me, Sinatra sounds like someone reading the

32

weather report. But even I could tell that Anne Ballard certainly wasn't no Barbra Streisand. Neither was she a Shirley Bassey, nor a Peggy Lee. In short, she wasn't a singer. Her voice was quite full and, wisely, she spoke the words rather than tried to sing them. When she did actually go for a note, her aim was terrible. But it didn't matter a toss. She was virginal and sexy at the same time, and there's nothing more exciting than a sexy virgin. I can't even remember the numbers she sang. I think she murdered a couple of Cole Porters and badly mauled Jerome Kern. But the audience loved her. At least, the male half of them did. When occasionally somebody, usually a woman, made her voice heard above the singing, she was intimidated into silence by three hundred freezing looks or, in one case, by having a pint of beer emptied on to her lap.

I had started to push my way towards Anne as she started to sing, but I gave it up after a couple of yards. A very large man had glared at me and then stepped on my foot. He kept his foot where it was threatening to crush my instep if I moved a muscle, so I stayed where I was. Just before the end of her last number, Anne saw me. At least, I assumed it was me she smiled at and half raised her hand towards. My assumption was confirmed a second later as the large man removed his foot and glared at me again.

'Jammy bastard,' he hissed.

I grinned at him to show there were no hard feelings, but he was already staring at Anne again, anxious not to miss a moment of her act. I tried to analyse what it was that riveted the attention of every male in the room. Sure she was sexy, but so was the barmaid if it came to that. Certainly the barmaid had bigger knockers, and there was an open invitation in her shrewd eyes and in the wide open front of her silk blouse.

Anne looked like everybody's sister, and you've got to be real kinky to fancy your sister. But fancy her they all did, in spite of the fact that in most cases the women they were with gave infinitely more promise of a successful and satisfactory roll. I decided that analysis was for the birds. Everybody fancied her and she fancied me. At least, she had hinted that way.

As I pushed my way through the crowd after she had finished, I felt a twinge of guilt about Mary. But she was out swinging somewhere and, being the bastard that I am, I never let my conscience get in the way of anything I want to do. And right now, I wanted to do Anne Ballard.

Another large man stood at the bottom of the stairs where she had disappeared after taking six bows to tumultuous applause. I started to mount the stairs, but he moved in front of me.

'Miss Ballard, please,' I said.

'Get lost!' he said.

'I think she's expecting me.'

He looked down at me from his six feet five inches. 'You've got to be kidding.'

'Business,' I said, playing it cool. He looked at me a moment longer, making up his mind. 'Get lost!' he repeated. To add a little weight to his argument he put a hand like a bunch of bananas flat on my chest.

I'm a mild mannered fellow by nature, and I dislike violence of any kind. Especially do I dislike violence that is directed towards me. Putting it another way, I'm a coward. My standard opening gambit if someone threatens anything physical is to beat a hasty retreat. I had just about decided that is what I would do when Anne appeared at the top of the stairs. There's something of the little boy in every man, evincing

34

itself in a desire to show off in front of the opposite sex. Here was this bruiser about to shove me heartily in the chest and, while normally I'd have allowed him to do just that, the fact that Anne was to be witness to the scene upset my metabolic balance to the extent that discretion and good sense took a jump out of the window.

When I was in the Service a number of hefty ex-army instructors had endeavoured to teach me judo and karate. They'd failed miserably. To me, a black belt was something for keeping up a dark pair of trousers. But two things I *had* learned. One was the way to kill a man with a stiff fingered jab in the side of the throat. But this seemed a little too drastic a ploy just to impress a bird. So I used my other gem of know-ledge in the noble art of self defence. Stated simply, this is never to give the other fellow an even break. Ninety-nine point nine per cent of the men who are going to use some muscle announce the fact beforehand. They threaten, they bully, and finally they take two seconds to weigh up the con-sequences of what they are about to start. Only then do they haul back and let fly. If you've got a nasty turn of mind like I have, this winding up period can be used to settle the argu-ment before it starts.

The other fellow had also seen Anne and, like me, he was gripped with the urge to impress. I was five inches shorter than he and his hand on my chest hadn't felt any real resistance. He weighed up the pros and cons carefully and, conscious of his physical superiority, he decided to thump me. But, like I said, this took time. Long before he had reached his conclusions, I had stepped back a pace and kicked him hard where it would do the most good. As far as he was concerned all further thought or action became superfluous.

I turned apologetically to Anne as he reeled back clutching himself and being sick down the front of his suit. She was looking sorry for him. 'He was going to thump me,' I said.

'You should have told him you were a friend.'

'I did. I think that's why he was going to thump me.'

I was aware suddenly that there were three more large men, each of whom could have taken Cassius Clay with one hand tied behind his back. My childish satisfaction at having downed the bully in front of my girl friend evaporated miraculously. One of the trio had now slipped on brass knuckles. I assumed he was the gaffer. I turned to him.

'He was going to thump me.'

'So are we,' he said companionably.

'He's a friend of mine,' said Anne quickly. 'Pete thought he was a trouble maker.'

The gaffer got a soppy look on his face as he turned to Anne. 'Is that right, Miss Ballard?' She nodded. He looked at me. Now he really wanted to work me over, but he managed a smile that nearly fractured his jaw.

'Sorry,' he said.

I decided to be magnanimous. 'A natural mistake,' I said. 'I'm glad to see that Miss Ballard is so well looked after.'

He managed to hold the smile in place, although his eyes were black with hate. 'We'd cripple anyone who upset Miss Ballard,' he said. I believed him implicitly.

Anne took my arm and devastated the three of them with a show of teeth. 'Thank you all so much,' she said. 'I hope Pete's . . . I hope Pete is all right. Good night.'

*   *   *

'How did you like my act?' she said in the car.

'Very much.'

'Why?'

'It's a good act.'

'But I can't sing.'

'Joan Sutherland can,' I said. 'But she'd die in there.'

'I know it,' she said. 'So what's so good about my act?'

'*You* are.'

'Sex?' she said.

I just managed to stop myself from saying 'Yes please', as I realised that she was still talking about her act.

'Virginal sex,' I said. 'It's a short supply commodity in these parts.'

She giggled, a sound which usually grates on my nerve ends, but which in this case only served to make me feel a little hornier than I did already.

'Where would you like to go?' I asked.

'Are you going to feed me?'

I had four pounds ten shillings in my pocket, but I took a chance. 'Of course.'

'You choose,' she said, settling back.

*　　*　　*

I chose Carlo's Place at the far end of the Fulham Road, where the food is good, the price right and the service friendly without being overwhelming. Halfway through the second course I began to deploy my troops.

'Who looks after your sister when you're working?' I asked, calling up the left flank.

'Nobody, she's quite happy on her own.'

37

'She lives with you all the time does she?' I enquired, gently alerting the right flank.

'Friday to Tuesday she stays with our aunt in Camden Town.'

For one blinding moment I couldn't remember whether it was Monday or Tuesday. Then it came to me, and I called up the whole bloody army and advanced with banners unfurled.

'She's away tonight then?' I said. I tried to throw the line away casually, but my aim was way off. It landed between us with a thump that rattled the crockery.

She glanced up at me through eyelashes that just had to be false, but I knew they weren't. 'That's right,' she said.

I had to do something to change the conversation fast. I turned round and casually waved my arm at the waiter. The waiter didn't see me, but I knocked my wine glass over and the contents emptied into my lap.

*   *   *

By the time we'd mopped it all up and spread a serviette over the stain on the tablecloth, we were on to the coffee and I was temporarily off the boil. I sat simmering through the coffee and was ready to cut the waiter's throat when he suggested liqueurs. Anne, bless her, declined and there was a banging of the table and a scraping of chairs as I galloped her out of the place, cursing the time it took to pay the bill.

*   *   *

I covered the Fulham Road in four minutes flat and parked in the forecourt of The Rabbit Warren. We both got out and I held her arm across the lobby, trying not to smirk at the two night porters, who watched us casually.

*   *   *

38

There are those among us who say that a girl who allows a man to tumble her the first time they go out is a tramp. I don't go along with this. You might as well say that a girl who doesn't allow a man to tumble her after they've been out a dozen times is automatically *not* a tramp. It's an argument that just doesn't hold water. If the basic attraction is there, it doesn't take a month to work out whether to hop into the sack or not. This is being dishonest with yourself and with your intended sackmate. Bed is only an extension of a natural physical attraction and, if the attraction is there, it's hypocritical to deny its fulfilment. That's how I looked at it, anyway. So I felt like a right idiot when Anne flatly refused to let me past the front door.

'Thank you for dinner,' she said, blocking the way as efficiently as a Harvard fullback. My face must have fallen six inches. She patted me on the cheek like someone consoling a desolate child.

'Cheer up,' she said. 'I'm not your type.'

It was such a basically stupid remark that I couldn't think of anything to say for a moment. I had been sitting on my hands all evening, and I'd had great difficulty in not misting up the cutlery with my heavy breathing. And now, here she was, as good as saying I didn't fancy her.

'Yes you are,' I managed to croak.

She looked at me steadily for a beat and I felt like a predatory rapist. I looked away and by the time I looked back at her, she'd gone, closing the door in my face.

* * *

It was the porters' turn to smirk as I slunk out of the building. I started the car, revving the engine savagely. I drove out of the

39

forecourt, narrowly missing a taxi which was coming in. I shouted an obscenity at the driver and was answered in kind. Right then I felt for Harvey Stubbs and all of the other men she must have left outside her front door. It was downright dishonest for a girl as sexy as she was not to come across. I recalled the thumping in the pub that I had nearly received on her behalf and felt even angrier.

*　　*　　*

I slotted the car into a space outside Mary's place and clumped my way upstairs. I tapped on the door of her apartment and tried to organise my face into a semblance of normality before she opened it. She finally opened the door, dressed for bed bed, as opposed to sex bed. Bed bed consisted of curlers in the hair, cold cream on the face, and the most sexless pair of shorty pyjamas imaginable; black I think, with white polka dots, or the other way round.

'Well?' she said.

I started to step into the flat and she jammed the door on to my foot. I must have looked surprised.

'I had dinner at the 'Durrel Arms',' she said.

The significance escaped me for a moment. So her date had fed her at a pub, I thought; she thinks *she's* got problems. Then the significance didn't escape me any longer. The 'Durrel Arms' was right opposite Carlo's Place. She'd seen me with Anne.

'It was business,' I said.

'So's this,' she said. She opened the door a little wider, then slammed it hard against my foot. By the time I'd finished hopping around, she'd shut it once more, this time for good. I limped downstairs, got into my car and drove home. For a Monday, the day had been about par for the course.

CHAPTER TWO

IT WAS raining on Tuesday, too. I fetched the newspaper and carried it into the kitchen to read while I was having my coffee. The Antonov story had made the front page this morning, due to the fact that a keen leader writer had started to ask how a man like Antonov could successfully operate in this country for ten years without being caught. It was a good question, especially as I knew that he had been under investigation for at least six of those years. Fortunately the newspaper man didn't know that or heads would have started to roll.

It seemed that during his ten years on the loose, Antonov had successfully corrupted countless atomic physicists, Foreign Office employees, Admiralty clerks, and two minor generals. Not a bad score, considering that the people who were supposed to prevent such things knew all about him.

It didn't really take much intelligence to work out that there was something fishy going on and I'd just about deduced what it was when the post arrived. There was a final demand from the London Electricity Board and an exhortation to do myself a favour and order *The Great Book of Art and Artists* at fifty per cent below list price, for selected customers only, this offer limited to three months. Fifty per cent below list price would have paid my electricity bill for the next six months. I dropped the letter in the wastepaper basket along with the final demand for the electricity. I didn't have the money to pay it and there was no point in having it lying around the flat where it could only depress me. The third letter was in a plain typed envelope. This one I opened last for no other reason than that it was at the bottom of the pile. In it was a newspaper cutting reporting the Antonov trial. Written in a broad hand in the margin were the words: *See me at your convenience*.

There was no signature, but I knew who it was from nevertheless. The handwriting was Max's and, that being the case, 'at your convenience' meant pretty damn quick, unless I wanted the Heavy Squad knocking down the front door.

I thought about me and Max while I was dressing. When I had worked for him, he had been omnipresent, a first-water *eminence grise*. It was he who had patted me on the back and sent me out on jobs that, even to think of them these days, curled my hair. I'd done those jobs for more years than I could remember, until even my pretty revolting standards could take no more. Then I had quit. He hadn't wanted to let me go. He didn't like anyone leaving the Service, unless it was feet first. But as my insurance against old age, I had started to build my '*dossier* on Max' in which I had outlined in detail some of the more unsavoury episodes he'd instigated. He had let me go in the end. He'd no alternative. I'd looked both ways before crossing the road for a while and hadn't wandered up any high places. But he really had let me go and, much to my surprise, there had been no repercussions. Apart from that painful incident six or seven months ago, he'd left me strictly alone, which was the way I liked it.

Unfortunately during this last episode, he had managed to get a severe edge on me which to some extent nullified the efficacy of my '*dossier* on Max'. He'd got me certified as criminally and incurably insane. If I knew my Max, my medical file was reposing right now in his filing cabinet and, unless I jumped when he said jump, I was going to be back in a padded cell before I could turn around.

So, if he said 'see me', I wasn't going to give him an argument. I got dressed and went to see him. He greeted me like the prodigal son. He's a small man physically, with thinning hair and a sharply defined face, all planes and angles. He has a thin, humourless mouth and very good teeth. His eyes are prominent and he's a permanent martyr to conjunctivitis. He uses eyedrops as frequently as another man uses a pocket handkerchief, pulling out a small bottle and squeezing the drops into the corners of his eyes. He did this as I sat across from him in his upper echelon civil service office. He blew his nose hard and put the bottle away. Then he looked at me, his eyes swimming.

'Good of you to come so promptly,' he said.

I kept my mouth shut. The best way to talk with Max is to say as little as possible. He has a remarkable knack of fashioning your own words into a noose which he uses to hang you.

'You read about Antonov?'

I nodded.

'Made you wonder a bit, I imagine?'

I hadn't really been all that interested, but I was forced to admit that I had wondered a bit.

'Thought we'd dropped a clanger?'

I admitted it had crossed my mind.

'Well we haven't.'

I knew he hadn't or he would not have had me up here to tell me about it.

'So knowing we haven't dropped a clanger,' he went on, 'What's your opinion of what has happened?'

I thought about it for a moment. Not about what had happened, because I was pretty sure I'd worked it all out over my coffee that morning, but about whether I should expound my theory. I'd long ago learned it was safer to volunteer nothing to Max. But time dulls the sharpest reactions, and whereas five years ago I'd not have opened my mouth, now I did, stepping in with both feet.

'I think you got on to Antonov five years ago and instead of eliminating him, you conned him into becoming a double agent. You've used him for the past five years to feed back duff information.'

'And?'

'And now his usefulness is at an end. He's probably been blown, and he's an embarrassment. So you put him away.'

Max smiled, showing perfect teeth. 'Half right,' he said.

'Which half?'

'The first. We turned him four years ago. He's been feeding them back the biggest load of codswallop you could imagine.'

'Now they've got wise,' I said.

'Now they've got stupid,' said Max. 'They're impressed with friend Gregori. They think he's no end of a bright eyed boy. He's held up as a number one example to all the new embryonic spies.'

He'd lost me, I'm afraid, and I told him so. 'So why lock him up where he's no good to anyone?'

'Because we've decided he can be more use to us working someplace else.'

'Like at home?' I asked.

'Like at home,' said Max. 'If they had him now, he'd be

44

given a section at least. Imagine that, John, a whole bloody section, and the leader is our man.'

It was a pretty fanciful idea and one that Max would have given someone's eyeteeth to achieve. And about here I started to get the trend. If I'd been sensible, I'd have trotted out of the office there and then and gone home and put my head in the gas oven. It would have been quicker and less painful. But I didn't. Like the idiot I sometimes am, I stayed and listened to Max confirm what I had already worked out.

'If we'd have left him free, they'd have been content to leave him here. He was doing good work, they thought, and there was no need to upset the *status quo*. So first we had to convince them that his usefulness here was at an end. So we pinch him. Now they're faced with one of their best men being out of action, while they'd like him working. The only way he can work is for them to get him back. The only way they can get him back is through an exchange.'

I was right on the button and now was the time to leave. I started to get to my feet.

'I've an authorisation to pay ten thousand pounds,' said Max.

I sat down again. Money does that to me at times; it paralyses the back of my legs. Max allowed me to sweat for a while before he continued. 'We can't be expected to swap him for any old rubbish,' he said. 'So we've got to find a man who ranks in their eyes equal with Antonov.'

'Yes?' I said.

'You did some pretty good work before you got cold feet,' said Max. 'They must have a substantial file on you somewhere in the archives.'

'I've done nothing for five years,' I said.

'Files are longer than that,' said Max. He was right of course. Somewhere in the Kremlin, or wherever it is they keep these things, there must have been a dossier six inches thick on John Smith. It would have gathered a fair amount of dust by now, but dust could always be blown off. I sat there chewing my lower lip for a while.

'Ten thousand pounds,' said Max.

'How long?' I asked.

'One month to set it up, three months to negotiate once they get you inside. Four months altogether.'

Twenty-five hundred pounds a month, more than six hundred pounds a week. It was pretty fair scratch, as long as you ignored the side issues. I decided to ignore them for a few minutes to see what happened. Max took my silence for partial acquiescence. 'I knew I could rely on you, John,' he said.

As I've said before, Max can be as wrong as the next man. I wouldn't have cut a hang nail for Max or the whole Service put together. But for ten thousand pounds, I'd cut my own throat which, as it turned out, I damned near did.

*   *   *

It seemed there was a trade mission going over to Moscow the following week. This was to provide my entry permit. Once there I would be contacted by various shifty individuals in Max's employ. They would spin a web around me and, when I was well and truly entangled, they would blow the whole thing to the KGB. There'd be a showy trial and I'd get fifteen years. The moment sentence was announced, negotiations would commence and, all being well, Max said, I'd be back in London four months and ten thousand pounds from now.

46

The actual details of what I was going to be arrested for, we didn't go into at this stage. Max in his infinite duplicity had decided the less I knew about what was going on behind the scenes, the more convincing I would appear. The prime requisite of a scheme like this was that I should appear absolutely genuine. John Smith, agent of long standing, quiet perhaps for the last five years, but still with an impressive record of espionage and counter-espionage. Truly a worthy swap for Gregori Antonov.

'You'll have to go down to the Farm for a few days,' said Max eventually.

'Why?' I knew the Farm of old. It was a place in the country kept by the Service for hiding, or doing away with people when the occasion arose.

'Briefing,' he said.

'Brief me here.'

'Can't, old son.'

'Why not?'

'Too many distractions,' he said.

'Distractions like what?'

'Birds. Things like that.'

I started to get suspicious. 'What's wrong with birds all of a sudden?'

'Nothing,' he said. 'So long as they're used just for sex.'

'So?'

'You're involved two ways in London and it's on a deeper level.'

Mary he knew about, so he had to be talking about Anne.

'How long have you had me lined up for this?' I asked.

'Couple of weeks.'

'You've been tailing me.'

'You're getting old, John,' he said. 'Time was when a tail couldn't hold you for two minutes without being spotted.'

'You've got a bloody nerve.'

'I know . . .' 'The Ballard girl worries me'.

'She worries me, too.'

'I know what you're like when you're not getting your oats,' he said. 'And from her you're not getting them.'

'Christ, I only met the girl yesterday.'

'Exactly,' he said. 'Can't allow you to get involved in any deep level courtship just before going out on a job like this. Might have a change of heart.'

He was right, of course, but he'd got well and truly up my nose by now. 'You can go and jump in the lake,' I told him. 'I'm not going down to the Farm.'

'At least down there you'll get your ration,' he said.

The Service kept a list of phone numbers which were used occasionally, as required. The girls who lived at the ends of these numbers were quite extraordinary. Not true whores, or so they told themselves. They slept around for money only if they could be convinced that they were doing their patriotic duty at the same time. Their true identities and backgrounds were kept well shrouded, but when I had been in the Service I had known two of them. One had been the wife of a senior civil servant and the other had been the girl friend of a junior minister. They were paid a small retainer by the Service, which arrived in their letter box in the guise of some obscure pension. And they were given bonuses whenever they were required to give their all for Queen and Country. If their domestic arrangements intruded on their duties more than three times in succession, they were quietly paid off. I never knew who the selection board consisted of, but whoever they were, they did their job well. The girls were lovely, intelligent, and marvellous in bed. When they eventually left the Service, whatever the reason, they did so discreetly with never a murmur of a come-back. I say they were marvellous in bed, because that is what I had been told. I'd never been important enough to warrant their professional services. Now, it seemed, I was. There had been one girl in particular I had met.

'Is Margaret still on the payroll?' I asked. They were all known solely by Christian names.

'Margaret has three children and weighs thirteen stone,' said Max. Five years was a long time.

I digested the Farm bit for a couple of minutes and I was finally forced to the conclusion that what Max was suggesting was the only sensible solution. With a major briefing on my back, I couldn't afford to get myself into a state about Anne Ballard. And if I did manage to storm the ramparts before I left for Moscow, then I was going to be in two minds about going at all. Mary, I wasn't worried about. Our affair had been going on long enough for me to leave her for six months at a stretch and then pick up again as though nothing had happened. I knew with Mary that if she met the right man, she'd marry out of my life and, while I dreaded the day, I knew that if it was going to come it would do so whether I was around or not.

So, having sorted out my immediate domestic life, and with the prospect of a gargantuan payday looming on the horizon, I threw caution to the wind and agreed to what Max outlined.

*   *   *

I had decided to leave Anne Ballard strictly alone, at least for a couple of days, so I called around at Mary's that evening, armed with a bunch of flowers and a new model vintage car for her collection. She opened the door and, seeing who it was, she turned and walked away. But at least she left the door open, so I went in and closed it behind me.

'Peace offering,' I said, holding out the flowers.

She took them from me without a word and went into the kitchen. I followed her in.

'Am I forgiven?' I asked.

She shook her head vigorously without turning round.

'Shall I work on it?' I said in my little boy lost voice. I thought for one moment she was going to shake her head again. But she didn't. She nodded almost imperceptibly. It was enough for me. I walked back into the living room, feeling ten feet tall, and started to unwrap her present.

*   *   *

Much later, when I was leaving, I told her I was going away for a while.

'How long a while?' she asked.

'Three or four months at least,' I said.

'Do I see you before you go?'

I shook my head. 'I don't think so.'

She looked at me steadily for a beat, then brought up her hand and laid it flat on my cheek.

'Take care,' she said.

And that was it. I left quickly before I burst into tears.

*   *   *

Max had given me a day to clear up before I went down to the Farm. I went to the office on Wednesday and reported to Harvey Stubbs that all was well.

He bounced to his feet. 'She took the twenty-five?'

'She took it.'

The cheque was still in my pocket and, although it was made out to cash, I had no intention of keeping it. Neither did I intend him to have it back. He would be more inclined to keep away from Anne if he thought she *was* fifteen and *was* pregnant. He came round the desk and proceeded to pound me on the back.

'Good old John. I knew you wouldn't let me down. Good old John.'

'I went to see her sing,' I said.

He pulled a face. 'Terrible.'

'They loved her.'

He spread his hands. 'I know it. That's why I ain't going to tell her to sling her hook. Working clients I need. But as far as I'm concerned, socially, she might as well be clapped up to the eyeballs.' Which suited me fine.

I returned to my own office and put the cheque in an envelope. I addressed the envelope to one of my favourite charities, the one devoted to the welfare of unmarried mothers.

Then I called in Miss Roberts. 'I'm going away,' I said. 'I'll be gone about four months.'

Her face started to fall. I caught it before it hit bottom as I handed her a cheque and she read the amount I had written on it.

'This will cover your salary, your holiday money, the office rent and anything else that comes up.'

She fingered the cheque as though it were going to vanish in a puff of smoke. 'Are you sure it's all right?' she asked. She had good cause. Yesterday if I'd written a cheque for that amount it would have bounced from here to Shannon. Max had promised to deposit twenty-five per cent of my fee in the bank that morning and he was far too dependent on me at this stage to let me down. The cheque would be good and I told Miss Roberts so. About then she started to get worried.

'Mr Smith, I hope . . . I mean . . . well . . . you're all right, aren't you?'

I nearly kissed her. She was worried that I'd been up to something illegal. I assured her that my new-found affluence was legitimate and she burst into tears. 'I'll miss you, Mr Smith,' she said, sniffing hard through her moustache.

'You've still got Mr Stubbs,' I said.

She brightened up a little, but not much. 'I'll keep everything exactly the way you like it. When you come back you won't even realise you've been away.'

I doubted that, but I let it ride.

I spent the rest of the morning tidying up, and telling Miss Roberts how to handle anything that might come up. Any new enquiries I told her to refer to Phil Bannister, an old mate of mine who could do with the work as much as I could have done yesterday. Finally I couldn't think of another thing to keep me busy. I stared hard at the telephone for ten minutes wishing it would disappear, thus obviating the necessity of welshing on myself. But it didn't, and I did. I called Anne Ballard.

'How did you know my number?' she asked.

'I was in your flat, remember?'

'What do you want?' she said, not unkindly.

'Take you out to dinner?' I said. There was a moment's pause.

'You're a glutton for punishment.'

'I'm a masochist,' I said.

'Pick me up at the pub?'

'No, thank you,' I said. 'I'll meet you at Carlo's Place.'

It was unlikely that Mary would see me twice in three nights. Anne agreed, and I hung up, feeling a bastard about Mary once more. But Anne had got her hook deep enough into me for me to want to settle it one way or the other. Either she'd have to start hauling in the line, or I'd remove the hook and cauterise the wound. I wasn't even sure which way I wanted it, but whichever it was going to be, it had to be settled and settled fast.

I said good-bye to Miss Roberts, who burst into tears again. I went home and packed a suitcase. I fished around in the wastepaper basket until I located the electricity demand. I wrote out a cheque, stuck it in an envelope and put the envelope in my pocket. The London Electricity Board had struck lucky. I even considered doing myself a favour and subscribing to *The Great Book of Art and Artists*, but reason prevailed and I let it stay in the basket.

Then, there being nothing else to do for the next few hours, I put my head down. I emerged a few hours later, bathed, dressed, locked up the flat and took the suitcase down to the car. There was someone lurking in the front seat of a car a few yards up the road, and I must have been an idiot not to have noticed him before, considering he'd been there for two weeks. But if I bothered to lose him now, Max would get suspicious. And anyway, Max had as good as told me to leave Anne alone.

So, because I don't like being told what to do, and because I get pig-headed when I am, I wanted him to hear that I'd taken no notice of his wishes in the matter. As I started the car and drove away, I gave the man behind me plenty of time to manoeuvre his own car out and slot into a space about two vehicles behind me. There he stuck all the way to Carlo's place. As I parked and went into the restaurant, I saw him reach into the glove compartment of his car and start in on some tired looking sandwiches. Life can be hell.

* * *

Anne arrived at eleven-thirty, by which time I was well stoned. Not so stoned though that I didn't get a lurch in my breastbone as she came in the door and across the restaurant towards me. Every man in the place watched her surreptitiously and, when I didn't even get to my feet as she sat down at the table, most of them would happily have cut my throat.

'Hi!' she said.

'Hi, yourself!' I countered. 'How's Pete?'

'He's worried,' she said. 'You really kicked him very hard.'

'I wasn't even trying,' I said. Here I was, on to the little boy act again, trying to impress. And tonight was my night for playing it cool, I had decided. So I pulled myself together, and I played it so cool the soup nearly froze over. Half way through the meat and veg., she began to figure me out.

'You're sulking,' she said.

'Nothing of the sort.'

'I liked it better when you were on the make.'

'You could have fooled me.'

'I didn't say I would have liked it better if you'd succeeded, I just said you were better company.'

'You don't have to worry any more,' I said. 'I made my pass and you saw fit to turn it down. It won't happen again.' It was the booze talking, of course.

'So why did you ask me to dinner?'

54

'To say good bye. I'm going away.'

I'd like to say that her face fell, but it didn't. She shovelled a mouthful of kebab into her mouth and, like the brave little girl she was, she didn't flinch.

'I'll probably be away about four months,' I said, continuing to flog a dead horse.

'Have fun,' she said.

Then I really did start to sulk. The whole evening gathered rapid momentum on its downhill run. By the time we reached the coffee, five minutes had gone by without a word being spoken. She weakened before me, as I was sure she would.

'Pass the sugar,' she said.

*   *   *

On the way back to her place I tried to rally the troops a little. I had been a firstwater shit all evening; so much so that even I felt a little guilty.

'You were right,' I said. 'I was sulking. I'm sorry.'

She patted my knee in a sisterly fashion. 'Apologies accepted,' she said. 'And I *am* sorry you're going away.'

'I could postpone it,' I said, grasping at straws.

'Not on my account,' she said.

*   *   *

And that seemed to be that. She rewarded me with a kiss on the cheek and a door closed gently in my face. Perhaps she needed a bit of brute force, I thought. Should I kick down the door of the apartment and rape her on the carpet. Then I remembered it was Wednesday and little sister was at home. This gave me the excuse I needed not to make a bigger fool of myself than I already had and, slinking out of The Rabbit

Warren for the second time that week, I climbed into the car and drove down to the Farm.

*   *   *

Agricultural things may go on at the Farm. If it is to provide a truly effective cover for what goes on inside the main building, I suppose they must plant and dig and slaughter sheep and milk cows, or somesuch. But it had never interested me and I had never bothered to find out. The only part of the place that had ever concerned me was the main farmhouse. It was a large, rambling building, with distorted corridors on three different levels, bedroom doors that didn't fit properly and low ceilings for bumping heads on. In the cellars were a couple of interrogation rooms of dazzling clinical whiteness, but from the ground floor up it was furnished in stockbroker rustic and was warm and comfortable.

If anyone was surprised at my arriving at three in the morning, they didn't show it. The door was opened by an anonymous young man who showed me to my room and then took my keys so as to put my car away. He told me I could breakfast at any time I wanted and, if there was anything I needed, would I be so kind as to ring the bell behind the bed. He called me 'sir', which was a fair indication of my general importance in the overall scheme of things. Later, I overheard him on the phone downstairs, reporting my arrival.

Just before I dropped off to sleep I wondered just what the hell I had let myself in for, apart from ten thousand quid. But I was tired, the bed was comfortable and my thought processes ground to a halt as I slipped over the edge of sleep and died for eight straight hours.

*   *   *

It was midday when I resurfaced, too late for breakfast. I rang my bell and a minute later the young man tapped on the door gently and came in. I suppose he did sleep sometimes, but I never caught him at it. I asked if I could have some coffee and he brought it to me while I was shaving. Lunch would be served in half an hour, he said, and there would be one other person apart from myself.

'Max?' I asked.

'No, sir,' he said, and left as unobtrusively as he had arrived.

I finished shaving and dressing and went downstairs. The main living room, which served as the dining room as well, was large and pleasant. The sun was streaming through the leaded windows, splashing pools of light on the highly polished, dark oak floor. The booze was located on the sideboard against the far wall. I crossed towards it and poured myself a healthy snort.

'Hello, Smith,' someone said.

I turned towards the door. There was no-one there. Then he stood up from where he had been sitting in a high backed wing chair. It was Leo Tamir. He looked as large as life, which was pretty bloody disturbing considering that I had personally shot him to death seven years before.

CHAPTER THREE

SEVEN YEARS earlier I had been a fully fledged, paid up, card carrying, prize winning operative for the Service. Admittedly the rot had already started to gnaw away at some of my nerve ends, but not sufficiently as yet for me to lift my fat ass out of the way of Max and his little schemes. That came a couple of years later. I was a one man team. I liked it that way. I didn't even trust myself overmuch, so I was quite incapable of trusting anyone else.

I had been in West Berlin on a job and was about to fly back to London when Max contacted me. It seemed there was a fellow who wanted to come over the Wall and our people wanted him very badly. I was to cross into the Eastern sector, make contact, and bring him safely back into the fold of democracy. It wasn't a difficult job technically, just highly dangerous.

I had a couple of men on the other side whom I used from time to time. It was reciprocal; they used me when they needed me. There is a certain level of the spy game where agents of opposing sides do each other small favours. It's quite a low level and the top brass, while being aware of it, are completely powerless to do anything about it. But Joe Red is doing the same job as John Blue; they're both overworked and underpaid; they both heartily despise the anonymous, desk-bound individuals who send them out on impossible tasks. So there is a certain affinity towards each other in spite of the fact that they work for opposite sides. In the past I'd used my men in the East to help smuggle over some unimportant people and they'd used me to ship back some undesirables we didn't want anyway. It was all very shifty and, as I said, only worked on low levels. The fellow Max now wanted me to bring over was not low level; he was extremely high. So my opposite numbers on the other side couldn't be expected to help. At least, not consciously. They needed to be conned into it. And a right royal conning it turned out to be.

I told them I wanted to get my hands on an East German railway worker who was passing forged ten dollar bills. They said fine, but could they please have Otto Heidler, who had come over the Wall a month before, leaving a wife, a mother-in-law and eleven children to be cared for by the State. The deal was arranged and, at the last minute, the man I wanted quietly dropped out of his usual domestic and social pattern and became the railway worker. He came across the Wall gift-wrapped and I bunged Otto Heidler across to them. Fat Otto was delighted to be going back, mother-in-law and eleven children notwithstanding. He had missed the whole bunch of them and had himself been trying to work out a way to get back to them. But such was the nature of my job at that time, I would have delivered him back anyway, even if he had screamed blue murder all the way. I was like that in those days.

The plan was then to shift my man out of West Berlin on the first available aeroplane; to get him well clear before the balloon went up across the Wall. But about here the whole thing started to backfire. My man dug his Germanic heels in and said he wouldn't leave Berlin unless his wife and two children were smuggled over the Wall to join him. He was immovable in this decision and, bar hitting him over the head and sending him air freight, there was nothing I could do about it. So I did the only thing left to me. At great personal risk to life and limb, I smuggled over his wife and two kids. This I had to perform all by myself. I couldn't get on to my regular contacts because that would have blown the identity of the man I'd just conned them into sending over.

Unfortunately they were already two jumps ahead of me, having found out that they had been duped. They didn't care about the wife and the children; they were only interested in the head of the family. So they allowed me to sweat a few days while I worked out a way to re-unite the family; then they allowed me to sweat some more while I carried out my plan. There were even some shots thrown at us to make the whole thing look real. They must have been laughing like a row of buckets, especially as they had sent Leo Tamir along behind us.

He spoiled the family reunion I had arranged by arriving five minutes after I had left and shooting the lot of them, kids and all. There was no one we could scream at for this bit of skulduggery; it was an occupational hazard. The only thing that lifted it out of the realm of the everyday was my part in it. For three days I had been living with the wife and the children and, bonded somehow by our common fear of discovery, we had grown closer together than we had any right to allow. She was a gentle, pretty girl of twenty-eight or thereabouts. The children, a boy and a girl, were seven and nine years old respectively. We had crouched in dirty cellars, slept under a common blanket, crossed a muddy frontier, and at one moment I had even started to entertain wild ideas about not delivering her back to her husband at all. But what with the children, and the fact that she was a very sensible girl to boot, I *had* delivered her to her husband and five minutes later all four of them were drowning in their own blood. And I developed a king sized needle.

I phoned Max and told him I wanted a month's leave. I didn't have any due to me, but he guessed what I wanted to do and, as it fitted in with his scheme of things, he happily granted my request.

It took me three weeks to locate and catch up with Leo Tamir. I did so finally in a disused garage five miles inside East Berlin. As an executioner he was ideal type casting; tall, colourless and very thin. His body seemed to be completely devoid of any flesh; just a thin layer of skin stretched tightly over an animated skeleton. He sidled into the garage, looking for the contact I had conned him into believing he was to make. I let him get one good look at me so that he would know why he was dying. In those days I considered myself a pretty dab hand with a firearm and I put two bullets side an inch each of his navel. He was rolling around on the floor, dying painfully, when I stepped over him and walked out. That was the last I saw of him. Three or four months later we learned circuitously that he was no longer with us, having been given a State funeral, third class.

*   *   *

And now here he was, seven years later, as large as life and twice as ugly. He still looked like an animated skeleton, only now the skin wasn't so tightly stretched. There was a wrinkle here and there, as though it had been badly dry cleaned somewhere along the line. I looked at him for a long moment, the bottle still poised over my glass.

'It must have been one of my off nights,' I said.

'Fortunately that wasn't the case with the surgeon they took me to,' he said. His English was almost perfect, with just a trace of an American accent buried somewhere not too deep. I held up the bottle.

'Drink?'

He shook his head and patted his stomach lightly. 'Thank you, no,' he said. 'I have trouble with my stomach if I am not careful.'

I remembered the two bullets I had placed there. 'Yes, you would.' I said. I finished pouring my drink and carried it across to a window seat where I sat and studiously studied the trees and fields through the window. The sun had gone in suddenly. Behind me Leo cleared his throat. It sounded like someone scraping their fingernails across sandpaper.

'We have things to discuss, Mr Smith,' he said.

I didn't turn round. Even after seven years the very thought of Leo Tamir made me want to throw up. Before I had ended his career, he had been hatchet man extraordinary for the East Germans. The little interlude which directly concerned me had been just another four notches in a gun butt that had already been sliced to ribbons. We knew of sixteen murders that could be laid at his door and there must have been God knows how many others. He had been the true professional in his day, working on the principle that loose ends can be woven into a noose, so cut the loose ends. The wives, girl friends or children of his victims were all loose ends as far as he was concerned, so they all went to his own private wall; butcher *par excellence* was Leo.

'We have things to discuss,' he said once more.

The view out of the window wasn't as impressive as I had first thought, so I turned towards him. 'What do you want?' I asked. 'Apologies?'

He looked at me blankly for a moment, then he grinned without humour.

'You are joking,' he said.

'You tell me.'

'Next week you are going to Moscow,' he said. 'There are things you must know about.'

'For instance?'

'It is my task to acquaint you with certain names, addresses and pieces of information which will be of use to you while you are there. They are designed to make your eventual arrest appear authentic.' His English wasn't so good after all; he talked like a page from the manual on How Not to be a Spy in Five Easy Lessons.

'Why you?' I asked.

'Because it is my job,' he said. 'I have been sent here specifically for this purpose.'

'Sent by whom?'

'My employers.'

'KGB?'

'CIA.'

So that was where he'd been for the last few years.

'What's the CIA got to do with this?' I asked, not keen to know the answer. I didn't like the CIA, they were too big. When an organisation has upwards of seventeen thousand agents in the field, it's natural that there should be slight deficiencies when it comes to servicing them. I'd known CIA men in the old days who'd stayed out in the field three times as long as anyone else because their Control had too many men to deal with and someone had mislaid their file. Max hadn't mentioned the CIA when he was giving me the deal.

'It's a joint operation,' said Tamir. 'Your department and the CIA.'

This made it worse; it conjured up visions of inter-departmental rivalries, petty jealousies and, above all, not letting one hand know what the other was doing. If I'd have had any sense I'd have quit there and then. Unfortunately the time for quitting had passed the moment that I saw and recognised Tamir.

'So discuss,' I said. And we discussed.

* * *

We talked over lunch and we talked all afternoon and into the evening. Or rather, he talked, and I only opened my mouth to shovel in food and drink and to ask an occasional question. One of these I asked fairly early on. How was it that Leo Tamir, who was supposed to be dead, was working for the CIA?

'I was very ill for a long time after our meeting,' he said, without particular rancour. 'My employers thought it advisable to announce my death. That way, when I returned to work, I would have the benefit of additional cover. After a year in hospital, I returned to the field.'

'Same job?'

'No. I'm afraid my taste for the old job had soured a little. My English was good, and I spoke three other languages, so I became an interrogator.'

That was like saying he had become fed up with killing people quickly, so he started killing them slowly. I started to dislike him even more than I had done originally, which wasn't easy.

'I worked at that for two years,' he said. 'And then I received this offer from the Americans.'

Just like that. He received an offer of employment from a rival firm, so he accepted. What price patriotism? I thought. But this thought only served to remind me of just how long I had been out of the game. In the old days, patriotism had been a dirty word.

'Your original employers couldn't have been overjoyed,' I said.

'They were extremely unhappy,' he said. 'They have tried to kill me on more than one occasion.'

It was a pity they hadn't succeeded, then I wouldn't have had to sit here looking at his animated death's head.

The instructions he gave me covered the broad outlines of what I was to do when I got to Moscow. Names and addresses were committed to memory, identification phrases were gone over, and along towards the end of the day I started to get very suspicious. But my suspicions needed airing in front of Max, not Leo Tamir, so I allowed him to plough on while I sat there soaking it all up and disliking him more each minute.

Finally it was bedtime, and Tamir disappeared upstairs with a glass of warm milk. The young man came into the sitting room to see me.

'Is there anything you'd like, sir?' he asked politely.

I thought for a moment about Max's extravagant promises to lay on a Service whore, should I feel so inclined. Then I decided that I didn't feel so inclined, so I bid the young man good night and went up to bed myself.

*   *   *

Leo Tamir was with me all the following day, retracing the ground he had already covered. I purposely made a couple of stupid mistakes so that I could watch him get the needle. He didn't. He corrected me with infinite patience and re-explained the point I had so obviously missed. Then he moved on to the next one. My suspicions were confirmed some time during the day and that evening I told the young man I wanted to make an outside telephone call.

He smiled apologetically. 'That's not permitted I'm afraid,' he said.

'I want to talk to Max,' I said.

'He left no instructions.'

'Take your pick,' I said. 'Either I call him from here, or I go down to the village and do it from there.'

His eyes flicked over me briefly, working out how much muscle he might have to use. It wouldn't have been much. He was a trained man, and a swift kick in the cobblers wouldn't have worked here like it did in Anne's pub. But then he decided that he'd better not damage the goods he was supposed to be looking after, so he excused himself politely and returned three minutes later.

'Max is on the line,' he said.

The phone was in the hall, a direct line to Max.

'What do you want?' he said.

'I want to see you.'

'What for?'

'I'll tell you when you get down here.'

There was a pause at the other end.

'Is it important?'

'Anything that could make me want to see you would have to be important,' I said. He muttered something unintelligible at the other end of the line.

'What did you say?' I asked.

66

'I'll come down tomorrow.'

'Before six,' I said. 'Or I won't be here.' And I hung up.

*   *   *

Tamir disappeared upstairs early again with his glass of milk. I'd not seen him eat or drink anything except warm milk for two days, and I began to think my aim seven years ago hadn't been as bad as I had thought. Seven years is a long time to nurse a sore tummy.

*   *   *

When I came down to breakfast the following morning, Tamir wasn't there. But there was a nervous young man sitting at the table alone. He jumped to his feet as I came in as though I were important. 'My name is Harcourt,' he said.

'Smith,' I said, helping myself to orange juice.

He started to smile, then looked embarrassed. 'Good morning Mr–er–Smith,' he said.

'Just Smith,' I said, sitting down.

'Yes, sir,' he said. 'When do you want to start?'

I hadn't the faintest idea what he was talking about.

'Why not now?' I suggested. He seemed relieved. He got to his feet once more and fetched a bulging briefcase from the sideboard. He sat down again and, rummaging in the briefcase, handed me a pile of multi-coloured pamphlets.

'This is our latest model,' he said. 'It's a diesel, of course, and we can deliver with clutch or brake band and drum steering. It has removable cylinder sleeves, variable governor throttle control, adjustable radiator shutter. It will deliver 85 per cent of its horsepower at the drawbar, or it will perform beltwork at one half pound per horsepower hour at rated load.'

'What is it?' I asked.

He looked at me with a slightly pained expression. 'It's the diesel multi-purpose Mark Ten,' he said. I must have looked extremely stupid. 'It's a tractor,' he said, nearly bursting into tears.

I glanced at the pamphlets. It *was* a tractor. 'I think you're talking to the wrong person,' I said. 'The farm's out there, I'm just a house guest.'

'You're Mr John Smith?'

I agreed that I was.

'You're going to Moscow next week?'

Again I agreed.

'Well surely,' he said, 'If you're going to demonstrate the Mark Ten, you've got to know *something* about it.'

So I was to be a tractor salesman. Max couldn't put me on the booze stand, or in lady's underwear. He'd given me tractors. That was something else I was going to have to talk to him about. But having crossed the initial hurdle, young Mr Harcourt really stretched out. He bombarded me with pamphlets, drawings, specifications, and enough technical data to fill a small encyclopaedia. It all went in one ear and a good part of it spilled out of the other. But enough of it stuck and by half past five, when Harcourt left, I was pretty conversant with the multi-purpose Mark Ten. I couldn't have pulled it apart and put it together again blindfolded, as I'm sure Harcourt could, but at least I knew how to start the bloody thing.

*   *   *

Max arrived on the dot of six, his eyes streaming. He was a city man, grass and trees doing terrible things to his particular brand of conjunctivitis. What with that and the fact that he hadn't wanted to come at all, he arrived in a foul mood. This suited me, because when he lost his temper he was inclined to become unsubtle.

He poured himself a small whisky, drowned it with soda and stood in front of the fireplace, his legs spread wide.

'Well?' he said.

'What about Tamir?' I said.

'What about him?'

'You didn't tell me he was here.'

'I didn't know,' he lied. 'The CIA said they were sending a man. They didn't say who.'

I let it ride, it wasn't all that important. 'What's going on?' I said.

'You know what's going on?' he answered a little warily.

'I bought your original scheme,' I said. 'I needed the money sufficiently for me to ignore some of the rough edges. The pay was good.'

'Bloody good,' he interjected. 'So what's the complaint?'

'Side issues.'

'Ah,' he said. He rocked back and forth for a few seconds trying to work out how much he could get away with not telling me.

'Big operation, John,' he said. 'Large appropriation. Got to show as many results as we can.'

'Sort of bonus,' I said.

He smiled with his mouth only. 'Exactly.'

I went to fetch myself a drink. 'I don't like it,' I said.

'You're not required to,' he said. 'It doesn't affect your part of the job.'

'Yes it does,' I said. 'You're asking me to make contact with a VIP.'

'Right.'

'A Russian VIP.'

'Right again.'

'And what happens to this VIP after he's been contacted by a British agent?'

'I don't think they'll shoot him,' said Max.

'Then they must be getting soft since I turned it in.'

'Yes,' said Max. 'They have eased up a bit. He'll probably get the salt mines or somesuch.'

'What exactly have you got against this poor slob?'

'Nothing,' said Max, surprised that I should ask. 'He works in a department of the KGB. He's not a Controller yet, but he's a bright lad and soon will be. Nothing like chopping down the tree while it's still an acorn.'

'It stinks,' I said.

'I know,' said Max. 'But as long as we had to fake something for you to get up to, I thought this was as good as anything and better than most.'

'*You* thought?' I asked.

'CIA actually,' said Max. 'Your man's an expert on American affairs.'

'So you do their dirty work now, as well as your own.'

'We co-operate,' he said.

'What have they got to do with Antonov?' I asked.

'Nothing.'

'Then how did they know what we were about?'

Max thought quickly. 'They had some information on Antonov. When they heard we'd pulled him in, they offered to let us have it.'

That was a bloody lie for a start; the CIA never volunteered anything.

'They didn't know Antonov was a double?'

'No,' said Max. He was lying every time he opened his mouth now. 'But we had to tell them of course.'

'Of course,' I said.

*   *   *

Then we moved on to this and that and, after twenty minutes, during which time he sweated a little more than normal, he plucked up enough courage to glance at his watch and say that he had to get back to town. I walked to the door with him and he shook me by the hand, saying it was unlikely that he'd see me again before I left. I watched him walk back to his car and saw the driver get out to open the door for him. It was a lady driver, a mousy looking thing from the motor pool, who obviously disapproved strongly of evening drives into the country. Just before Max stepped into the car I shouted at him from the front door.

'I thought you said I could get laid down here,' I said.

He stopped, halfway into the car, and I saw him glance sideways at Miss Mouse. He stepped out of the car and walked back towards me. I suppose I should have met him halfway, but I didn't. When he was a good ten feet away from me I spoke again, just as loudly. 'There's no one here except Leo, and I don't fancy him.'

He reached me, his mouth a thin, straight line. I smiled at him broadly.

'Do you really want a woman?' he asked.

'I don't know till I see her, do I?' I said.

He sighed. 'All right,' he said. 'Tomorrow.'

He walked back to his car and Miss Mouse. Just before he got in I called to him again. 'A big redhead,' I shouted. He didn't acknowledge it. He got into the car quickly and the driver slammed the door after him. She marched round the front of the car, and as she was about to get in to the driver's seat, I delivered my parting shot. 'With tits,' I yelled.

The engine started up with a snarl of disapproval, and I watched the car until it disappeared between the chicken house and the barn, on the way out. Then feeling childishly pleased with myself, I went back in.

*   *   *

At dinner, Tamir appeared for the first time that day. He sat there sipping warm milk while I tucked into soup, meat and veg., the lot. With it I sunk a whole bottle of very good wine, capped the whole thing with three large brandies, and then went to bed. I slept like a log until half past five.

*   *   *

The dawn is a cold, lonely thing. It is not a time for constructive thinking. On the rare occasions when I wake up with the sun, I get up straight away rather than lie in bed and reflect on my problems. This morning I reflected and it was a pretty murky exercise. I decided that my feeling of well-being of the previous evening had been built on a liquid foundation, and now the whole thing was on the point of running down the plughole, taking me with it. But I was deeply committed by now and, if I had tried to wriggle out, Max would have become very nasty. And a nasty Max has to be seen to be believed. I decided I was better off taking my chance with the Russians.

I got up about seven and went for a walk. There was nobody downstairs when I went out and, by the time I came back at half past eight, the young man in charge had done everything bar call out the Marines. He'd phoned Max, he'd made discreet enquiries at the local police station, and he'd ordered half a dozen men in London to start looking for me. His relief at seeing me walk in the door only just outweighed his desire to cut my throat for causing him to get into such a state.

'Morning,' I said. 'What's the excitement?'

He pinched back his first remark and tried to smile at me. 'You're not supposed to leave the farmhouse,' he said.

'You should have told me.' I helped myself to some bacon and eggs and sat down at the table. 'What's on the agenda today?' I said. 'Tractors or Leo?'

'Political history,' he said primly.

'You're kidding,' I said. But he wasn't. At half past nine a man named Greeley arrived and I spent the day learning about the people I would have known about already if I hadn't quit the Service five years before. So-and-so now ran the Middle East office, having succeeded whatsisname who had been put in charge of the American Bureau; a man at the Italian Embassy was always a good bet if you wanted something leaked to the Russians; Carey, a second secretary at the US Embassy was the local head of the CIA; and so on and so forth. This went on through lunch and up until tea time, when Greeley packed his case and left.

*　　*　　*

I was pouring myself a large drink when Leo Tamir appeared. He probably didn't know, but I thought I'd ask him anyway.

73

'I've been given a lot of information today,' I said.

'More tractors?'

'People. An A to Z on who does what on the Moscow spy scene.'

'Necessary information,' he said.

'Too necessary,' I replied. 'I'm not in this for glory. If anyone asks me anything, I shall tell them. Nobody's going to have to pull any of *my* fingernails.'

'Then you must assume that the information that has been given you is designed with that in mind.'

'I'm being underpaid,' I said. 'Not only am I doing the job I was told I would be, but I'm spreading fringe benefits round like there was no tomorrow.'

'Please?' said Leo.

'First there's the man you've been briefing me on. The poor slob who's to be contacted by a British agent. And now there's half a dozen other pieces of choice information which I'm supposed to divulge.'

He pulled his mouth back, exposing his teeth. I think he thought he was grinning. 'If you have enough information to give away, they may grow tired before they can get you to give away the true purpose of your visit.'

It figured in a roundabout sort of way. The stuff I now knew would keep my interrogators busy for a couple of weeks. If I provided them with sufficient pseudo-genuine information, they might accept my cover without peeling off the last layer.

*   *   *

Over dinner Leo grew quite locquacious. He told me how he had gone to America and spent a year there engaged in what amounted to total recall of his ten years in the service of the

74

East Germans. The number of people he must have sent to the wall during this opening up of his mind would have been impressive by most standards. But for his career it was an anti-climax. He had merely taken his own finger off the trigger and aimed the gun for someone else.

'Do you sleep nights?' I asked.

'My stomach gives me trouble,' he said.

'Not your head?'

He looked at me for a moment, not understanding. Then he got it. 'You mean conscience,' he said. I nodded. 'No,' he said. 'It was a job like any other. I did it as best I knew how.'

'But you enjoyed it,' I said.

He shrugged indifferently. 'I never considered whether it was to be enjoyed or not. It was just a job.'

That was even worse. If he had been a sadist and had got a kick out of murder, it would have been understandable, if not commendable. But indifference put it on a completely different level. I called him a very rude name and left the table.

I was crossing the hall on the way upstairs to bed at the same time as our young man was opening the front door. He stood aside politely and a girl came into the hall. She was tall, very fair, and thin. She had muscular legs that looked as though they could squeeze the life out of you if she ever got a good hold. She was everything I didn't like in a girl, and this was confirmed a moment later when she spoke to the young man. 'Max asked me to come down,' she said.

She had a flat, nasal intonation in her voice which set my teeth on edge. Max knew my taste in women and he must have gone to great pains to find this girl. It was his way of paying me back for last night. As she came across the hall to say hello, I mumbled something fatuous and fled upstairs. It was just one more indication of how long I'd been away; Max *always* had the last snigger.

*   *   *

I spent four more days on the Farm. I talked with Leo Tamir some more and had two more visitors from London. One of them tried to show me how to work a small transmitter-receiver. I told him to stuff it; I was taking no radio sets to Moscow. There was a hurried phone conversation with Max, and the man left in high dudgeon, taking his radio with him.

The other visitor brought my documents. There was a passport, well used, a National Insurance Card, a driver's licence, a Diners' Club Card and a membership card to the Playboy Club. All these were made out in the name of Harrison King. Then there were a couple of photographs of an anonymous looking woman with two kids, and two personal letters that a man like King might have been expected to keep. To cap this do-it-yourself spy kit, there was a wallet containing dirty photographs and a packet of french letters. I decided I didn't much like Harrison King. But I was obviously going to have to live with him for the next few months, so I took the large file on my new found background up to my room, where I read it carefully, getting to know myself as well as I could.

*   *   *

On Monday morning, bright and early, a car called for me and, with a suitcase full of clothes that I normally wouldn't have been seen dead in, I was driven to Gatwick Airport.

At the airport I met some of the other delegates to the Trade Conference. They were about equally divided between dedicated men, who were determined to return with order books crammed, and the others, whose dedication lay solely in having a ball during the next two weeks while they were away from hearth and home. I gravitated towards this bunch who already, at ten thirty in the morning, were well on the way to getting smashed on airline champagne.

The aircraft was chartered, and my half of it swung vigorously all the way across Europe. After half an hour the hostesses refused to come up to our end of the aeroplane at all and we were forced to collect our own booze from the galley. This we did with inexhaustible enthusiasm.

*　　*　　*

Before we knew it, the captain, who had wisely remained in the driver's seat for the whole journey, announced that we were approaching Moscow.

*　　*　　*

The liquor I had consumed over the past few hours evaporated suddenly. The fun was over, let battle commence.

CHAPTER FOUR

LOOKING BACK on the whole Moscow bit, it's a bloody miracle that I managed to stay alive for more than forty-eight hours. The fact I *did* stay alive was not due to any particular ability of mine. Rather it was a long series of errors of judgment and execution by everyone concerned. I was merely a pawn, to be shoved this way and that, in the hope that I could be made to cause as much damage as possible before someone from the other side moved his queen and swatted me from the board.

*   *   *

It was dark when we touched down at the International Airport at Sheremetevo, about eighteen miles from Moscow proper. There was an official welcoming party of minor state officials, and we were hurried through the airport formalities with a haste that was almost indecent. Our entire party was bundled into a fleet of Ziv limousines, with one Intourist guide to each car. The drunken bunch I was with drew an attractive, serious faced young girl, who spoke better English than I did. Ideas of extra curricular activities entertained by any of our party in her direction were quickly squashed when Harbottle, an aggressive North Country idiot, laid a sweaty hand on her knee. She blasted him with a stream of Russian delivered in a tone cold enough to take his arm off above the elbow. As he snatched his frostbitten hand away, she switched back to English, without batting an eyelid, continuing at the point at which she had been interrupted.

She pointed out with pride the vast building programme which was gobbling up the outskirts of the city. Huge, multi-storied blocks of apartments, hung with scaffolding and topped by cranes, stuck up against the night skyline. Nearer the centre of Moscow, the scaffolding had disappeared and the same buildings were occupied and blazing with light. Then we were in Moscow proper, with its wide, straight streets. Here, the buildings were not so uniform in design as the workers' apartments on the outskirts; here there were still relics of pre-revolutionary architecture. This was the first time in Moscow for me, and I managed to find enough respite from my problems to show a reasonable interest in my surroundings.

The hotel was a genuine piece of Victoriana. The room I was eventually shown to on the fourth floor was large enough to hold a diplomatic reception. The ceiling was so high as to be almost out of sight, and the furnishings were comfortably ugly. There were heavy plush curtains, over-stuffed armchairs with dainty antimacassars, and a huge iron bed with a feather mattress deep enough to drown in. There was a connecting bathroom, with a hot water geyser that looked efficient enough to launch the entire hotel into orbit. There was a telephone and a pile of official notices in five languages. There was also a small printed notice in English welcoming me, as a member of the Trade Delegation, to the USSR. In small letters at the bottom it informed me that anything I wanted while I was in Moscow, I was to refer to my Intourist representative. I wondered what the serious young lady would say if I told her that I wanted to get arrested for spying. She would probably have found it as unbelievable as I did.

*   *   *

There was some sort of a wingding laid on for us that evening, and after a suitable time had been given to us for washing and changing, we reassembled in the lobby of the hotel.

We were bundled into the fleet of limousines once more and, accompanied by our young Intourist guide, were driven across Moscow to the monolithic pile that housed the Overseas Trade Centre. The booze consumed on the aeroplane that day had, by now, started to take its toll and my group was looking a very sorry bunch of high powered sales executives. Even the amorously inclined Harbottle was subdued, and the sight of our guide in a neat little black dress with discreet decolletage, did nothing to revive his spirits.

The party, if it could be so called, was held in a vast room into which they seemed to have crammed the entire population of Moscow along with diplomatic representatives from five different embassies. I think the Big Man himself was there, but I couldn't be sure; since the exit of Khrushchev I've never been quite sure who it is and, anyway, all Russian politicians look the same to me. There was a sprinkling of large Russian wives, and some slimmer women who obviously came from the embassies; there was a mess of interpreters, smooth eager young men in ill-fitting lounge suits; there were photographers and reporters from the accredited news agencies; and there was half a ton of caviare and a seemingly inexhaustible supply of champagne and vodka. I spent three-quarters of an hour talking to four large Russians about the multi-purpose Mark Ten.

Fortunately I had to do this through an interpreter, so the more glaring holes in my discourse could be laid at his feet as examples of bad translation. Even so, I thought they looked at me a little strangely when I was explaining the slip differential. But, on the whole, the discussion passed off reasonably well.

They excused themselves after a while, when they went to discuss the merits of a new type of combine harvester, and I found myself alone for the first time since I had arrived at the party. Not wanting to get involved in another technical talk, I side-stepped two more men who were dragging an interpreter towards me, and pushed my way through to the bar. I ordered three vodkas and, pouring them all into one glass, I started to make my way to a distant corner of the room where I imagined I might be able to sit out the remainder of the evening undisturbed. I didn't make it. Halfway across the room, I felt my elbow grabbed from behind. Turning, I saw a short, dapper man, with sandy coloured hair and rimless spectacles.

'Comrade King?' he enquired politely. I confirmed that I was indeed Comrade King, and he stuck out his hand.

'Alexei Alexandrovitch,' he said. I shook his hand. It was dry, yet still managed to give the impression that it was clammy. I decided I didn't like him.

'You are the representative of the tractor people?' he asked.

'Multi-purpose Mark Ten,' I said. 'We can deliver with clutch or brake band and drum steering. It has removable cylinder sleeves too.'

'Interesting,' he agreed.

'It will deliver eighty-five per cent of its horse-power at the drawbar.'

'Very interesting,' he said. 'What else will it deliver?'

'When performing beltwork it will deliver one half pound per horse-power hour at rated load.'

He nodded a couple of times as though he knew what I was talking about.

'Will it deliver Vladimir Karkov?' he said finally.

I nearly asked him what the hell was a Vladimir Karkov. There was nothing about one in my pamphlets. Then through the booze came a flash of light. Vladimir Karkov was the man I was supposed to put the big finger on, the bright young man of KGB who was an expert on American affairs and would one day grow up to be a Controller. Except that he wasn't going to be allowed to grow up at all if Max and the CIA had their way. Three hours I'd been here and already they were sharpening the chopper.

'No doubt we could adapt the basic model to deliver anything you'd care to ask for,' I said.

'Later this evening,' he said. I looked around the room and the number of people in it. Then I looked back at him. 'It is a little crowded,' I said.

He sidled closer to me. He had halitosis. 'When this is over, come to forty-four Kotelnicheskaya street, apartment seventeen.'

'Which street?'

'Kotelnicheskaya,' he said.

I couldn't even pronounce it, let alone find my way there.

'Write it down,' I said.

'Too dangerous,' he hissed. He pronounced it again, syllable by syllable like a teacher taking a four-year-old through a primary reader. I must have got it eventually, because suddenly he wasn't there any more. He slapped my back, causing me to slop my drink, and with a hearty 'Good night, Comrade,' he was gone.

His place was taken by an earnest young man whose only interest in tractors was as a means of introducing himself. Once that had been established, we got on famously. He wanted to know about Western authors. Did I know the work of Ernest Hemingway? I told him that old Ernie and I had practically been born in the same bed. Had I read *The Sun Also Rises?*

'*Read* it? The hero was based on me,' I said.

He looked sympathetic. 'It must be terrible to be impotent,' he said.

I agreed that it had its disadvantages and resolved to read *The Sun Also Rises* as soon as I got home. We had covered Galsworthy and Chesterton and touched on Maugham, all bosom friends of mine, before I was dragged away by an interpreter to extol the virtues of the multi-purpose Mark Ten to a group of yokels up from the Urals. A couple of hours later the party broke up. We were picked up again by our Intourist guides, who shepherded us into neat little bundles and drove us back to the hotel. There we were bidden a polite good night, indicative of the fact that we were supposed to retire to our rooms and remain there until we were fetched the following day.

* * *

On every floor of every hotel in Russia there is a big woman who sits at a desk in the corridor. The desk is strategically placed so that she can see the doors to all the rooms and the stairs as well. I don't suppose it really is the same woman, but it might just as well be. From her eyrie she is supposed to command the efficient running of the floor. Maids, messengers, waiters are all summoned by her, and report back to her after they have performed their duties; towels, linen, keys are all organised by her. She also serves very well the purpose of keeping an eye on the comings and goings of the guests. She certainly phones down any unscheduled movements to the reception desk and it's an even money bet she's got her own hot line direct to the KGB. So subterfuge was in order if I was to keep my appointment.

I asked for, and received, a bottle of vodka and, nursing it tenderly, I enquired from her the room number of my good old pal Harbottle. We argued back and forth for a couple of minutes until she got the gist of what I was asking. Rigid with disapproval at this obvious example of drunken Western decadence, she phoned down to Reception and ascertained that Harbottle was on the third floor, the one below mine. She wrote the room number down because, being a stupid idiot who didn't speak a word of Russian, I couldn't be expected to understand what she was saying.

Thanking her profusely, I tottered off towards the stairs, giving a creditable imitation of a man who was three parts stoned and was about to complete the course. This part wasn't too difficult, because I *was* three parts stoned. The rest was simple. I just continued to walk down the stairs until I reached the ground floor, where I strolled across the lobby, like a man who had every right to, and out of the front door. The two women behind the desk didn't even look at me.

Once I got outside, my troubles really started. There were no taxis and, even if there had been, I wouldn't have taken one. Neither did I have any idea in which direction I was supposed to go. A hundred yards from the hotel I stopped a man and tried to pronounce the name of the street I was looking for. It took me five minutes to get it over to him that I wanted Kotelnicheskaya Street, by which time we'd gathered quite a

crowd. Fortunately, among the interested spectators was a
student whose command of English, while not being by any
means fluent, was at least comprehensible. He started to explain how I should get there, and then he got into an argument
with the man I had stopped as to the relative merits of taking
first left and second right, as opposed to second left and first
right. Luckily they sorted it out before the police arrived to
break up an illegal gathering. I gave them the bottle of vodka I
was still clutching to share between them and, as I left, they
were just starting another argument as to who deserved the
lion's share.

Forty-four Kotelnicheskaya Street was an old, brownstone
apartment building, sandwiched between an office block and a
depressing looking clothing store. I mounted the steps to the
lobby and was striking matches, looking for the bell push of
apartment seventeen, when Alexei Alexandrovitch grabbed
my elbow for the second time that evening, pulling me back
into the darkness of the hall. Coming out of the dark like he
did, he scared the life out of me and it was only by hanging on
to my tattered nerve ends that I refrained from bolting back to
the security of the hotel. As it was, it took me half a minute to
pull myself together and listen to what he was telling me.

It seemed that Vladimir Karkov had a mistress. There was
nothing illegal or even indiscreet in this. He was an unmarried
man with normal appetites and the KGB were only concerned
with his private life insofar as it reflected on his work for the
department. The girl in question was apparently well cleared
for security and the arrangement was satisfactory to all parties.
Up until now. Alexei had made a phone call to Vladimir,
purporting to be delivering a message from his girl friend to the
effect that she was in serious trouble, and would he please meet

her right away at apartment seventeen, forty-four Kotel-nicheskaya Street. He was due here in five minutes. The ruse was simple to the point of stupidity; it had the stamp of a second rate melodrama. And about here I began to question the validity of the statement that Vladimir was a bright young man who would go far. If he was *that* bright he would have smelled a trick of some sort.

'What if he phones his girl friend to check you out?' I asked Andrei.

'She is out of town.'

'You're sure?'

'She was phoned three hours ago and asked to meet Vladimir in their dacha thirty miles from Moscow. There is no telephone there.'

I hastily tried to think of another objection that would warrant my calling the whole thing off, but I couldn't. 'What am I supposed to do with him when he arrives?' I asked.

'Nothing,' said Alexei.

'What do you mean, nothing?'

'Just that. He will do all that is necessary.'

I had a quick vision of Vladimir pulling out a gun and shooting holes in me. But Alexei was way ahead of me.

'He never carries firearms,' he said.

'How do you know what he does when he's rescuing damsels in distress?'

But Alexei was insistent. 'He never carries firearms.'

He gave me the key of apartment seventeen and pointed me towards the stairs.

'Good luck,' he said. Suddenly I was alone and scared gutless.

Apartment seventeen was on the second floor. The building

was silent except for the muffled sound of a radio from one of the floors above me. I located number seventeen and let myself in. It was a spacious three bedroomed apartment of the old style which reflected the Russian passion for high ceilings and lots of elbow room. It was completely empty of any furniture, provided you discounted a battered, upturned packing case in the centre of the main room. I toured the apartment quickly. In the old days the first thing to do in a situation like this had been to make sure of your line of retreat. Always locate and check the way out, whether you thought you would need it or not. It took me thirty seconds to locate and check the fact that, in this instance, there wasn't a back way out. There was only the one door into the apartment, the one I had come in by. If Vladimir and I both decided that we had had enough, then we were going to trample each other to death on the way out.

After that, there seemed nothing left to do but sit and wait. Not the least unnerving thing about the whole bit was not knowing what I was waiting for. I knew that Vladimir Karkov would come hot footing it to rescue his girl friend, but rescue her from what? If Alexei had told him she was being raped, then in spite of his apparent dislike of them, he'd likely arrive bristling with firearms. With my non-existent command of the Russian language, I was going to be bleeding all over the floor before I could set him straight. On the other hand, if Alexei had concocted some milder type of story, where was I going to be left when he arrived and started to ask me questions? It was all very well for Alexei to say do nothing, leave it all to Vladimir, but Alexei wasn't going to be here, and I was. I decided that speculation was for the birds and sweated out the remainder of the time with my teeth chattering. I'd like to have blamed it on the cold, which it undoubtedly was. But not that cold.

Alexei's timing was dead on. Five minutes to the second Vladimir Karkov arrived. If he had come by car, I didn't hear it. The first sound I heard was that of hurried footsteps coming up the stairs. There was a moment's pause while he located the door of the apartment, and then the door bell rang. I remained where I was, sitting on the packing case facing the door, and wishing I was twelve thousand miles away. After a pause, the bell rang again, and a few seconds later the door started to open slowly. There was sufficient leaklight from the street lamp outside for me to see him pretty clearly. He was wrapped up against the cold in a fur collared overcoat and a fur hat; but I could still see enough of him to recognise him again if I had to. He was about forty years old, a fact of which I was already aware. He had a fine-boned face and dark, bushy eyebrows. There was a healthy growth of whisker on his upper lip which didn't quite hide a mouth that looked hard enough to break rocks. It was difficult to see his eyes in this light, but I found out later they were grey and flat like a Russian winter.

He saw me when the door was half open and he stopped, staring straight at me. Then he said something fast in Russian. It was obviously some sort of question and, not understanding a word, I kept my mouth shut. Then he stepped across the threshold and repeated the question. This time there was an edge of anger in his voice. I thought I'd better contribute something and, being unable to think of anything particularly witty, I fell back on the Englishman's standby. 'It's chilly tonight,' I said.

I might as well have said I'd just flown in from Pluto, so great was the effect. He stiffened visibly, right down to his toes. His eyes swept the apartment quickly, looking for my flying saucer perhaps. Then they settled on me for a full ten seconds. It seemed like ten days. Then he turned abruptly and ran down the stairs. I heard the outside door slam hard behind him, and I was alone once more with only the upstairs radio to keep me company.

And that seemed to be that. I was obviously doing nobody any good hanging around getting colder by the minute. I stood up and waved my arms about for a few seconds to restore my flagging circulation. Then I followed Vladimir out of the apartment. I left the door open and the key in the lock. What happened to it was none of my business. There was no one in the street outside and, turning up the collar of my inadequate overcoat, I trudged back to the hotel.

The large woman on my landing glanced up at me as I emerged from the elevator. If she knew that I had been anywhere other than to visit my old pal Harbottle, she didn't show it. I could feel her eyes boring holes in my back as I walked to my room and let myself in. I tried a tentative 'good night' in her direction, but it was met with stony indifference, her rimless spectacles making it look as though she had two large holes drilled in the front of her skull. I slammed my bedroom door hard, hoping it would annoy her and started to get ready for bed. Fifteen minutes later I was sound asleep, engulfed in my feather mattress.

*   *   *

It took six hours for them to draw together all the strings and weave them into what amounted to my noose. That made it half past five in the morning when they came for me. There were four of them, two in the room and two more hovering about outside. They were very polite and didn't throw their weight about. Not that I gave them cause. As soon as the light snapped on, I was wide awake and already halfway out of bed.

'Mr King?' asked the elder of the two men in the room. I concurred. 'Please, you will come with us.'

I made the requisite noises of bewilderment trailing into protest and back into bewilderment. All this while I was getting dressed, watched with evident disinterest by the older man, while the younger stood just inside the door, hands deep in pockets, ready to blow my head off.

As I was ushered out by these two, the other pair, who had been waiting outside, came into the room and proceeded to dismember my belongings. My large Russian lady was still sitting behind her desk, her expression no more disapproving than it had been before. No doubt, in her mind, sneaking out in the night clutching a bottle of vodka was just as bad a crime as that which caused the KGB to collect me at crack of dawn. Perhaps she even thought that was the reason they *were* collecting me. I felt like goosing her or sticking out my tongue, anything to get beneath that monolithic shell. But by the time I had made up my mind not to, it was too late anyway. I was shuffled across the deserted lobby and out into the Moscow dawn.

If I had thought it was cold before, now it was really something to write home about. My overcoat, designed for a London winter, was no match for its Moscow equivalent. The wind carved straight through to the bone so quickly that by the time I had been escorted across ten feet of pavement and bundled into the back of an anonymous looking black car, my teeth were chattering like castanets. Privately, I was delighted, because they would have been chattering anyway. This way I could afford to let them without losing face.

The ride to God-knows-where took twenty-five minutes and was conducted for the most part in silence. I made one half-hearted protest, babbling something about the British Embassy, but I only did this because I imagined it was expected of me, and not because I thought it would do any good. Here, I was right; it did no good whatsoever, and I spent the remainder of the journey preparing myself for the nastiness that was to follow.

The building outside which we disembarked was as anonymous as the men and the car. There were no guards on the door, and no official signs or notices proclaiming its function. It was just another building, like all the others in a nondescript street. This fact gave me no encouragement at all. There are buildings like this all over the world where the really nefarious things take place, things far too messy to be conducted in official places. I was hustled up the steps and through a door that opened in front of us when we were still four feet away from it. I had a momentary glimpse of a mournful looking man standing behind the door, as I was marched across a grey, stone floored hall, and through a door on the far side. This gave on to a corridor with half a dozen doors leading from it.

My escort knew exactly where they were going. They ignored the first three doors, then jerked me to an abrupt halt outside the fourth. The younger man opened it, and the elder indicated with a nod of his head that I was to go through. I did so and the door was closed quietly behind me. I didn't hear a key turn, but when I tried the handle a moment later, the door was locked solid. The room was furnished lower echelon civil service, and I could have been in the office of any ministry in practically any damn country in the world. There were two standard filing cabinets, a two-drawer wooden desk with one chair behind it and one in front. Against the wall was a small table which in London would have held the tea making paraphernalia, but here in Moscow they obviously took their tea drinking seriously; on the table were two dirty glasses and an empty vodka bottle. The walls were grey, like the floor and ceiling, and were covered with a slight film of condensation. Although the room was a good twenty degrees warmer than it was outside, it was still bloody cold.

I wasn't sure what was expected of me, so I sat on one of the chairs to wait it out. But in case anyone was watching me, and not wanting to look as scared as I was, I reversed the chair and straddled it, trying to behave nonchalently, as if this sort of thing happened to me every day; and even if it didn't, I was wrapped up and protected by my obvious innocence. I don't know whether anyone *was* watching, but two minutes later the door opened quietly and Vladimir Karkov walked in.

This was a turn up for the book and no mistake. My rendezvous with him was designed solely to plot his downfall and now here he was, as large as life, and obviously acting in an official capacity, about to start asking me questions.

I remained seated while he closed the door behind him. He looked at me, a little sadly I thought, for a long moment. Then he sighed gently through his moustache. He pulled the other chair out from behind the desk and sat down so that he was facing me, his face a few inches away from mine. He continued to regard me stolidly for another thirty seconds, during which time I tried not to blink, and failed three times.

'What's it all about?' he said suddenly. It was a surprise; he looked so bloody Russian that I had expected at least the trace of an accent. There was none, unless you could classify minor Oxford as an accent. It was no good my pursuing the outraged

British Citizen with Karkov, so I didn't bother. I tried the innocent tack.

'What's all what about?'

'Why was it arranged that you and I should meet in Kotelnicheskaya Street?' he said. Then, before I had time to open my mouth, he answered his own question. 'No,' he said. 'Not why. I know the reasons. What I now must know is what follows.'

Not knowing, I said nothing. After a pause he continued. 'In situations such as this your people will, one, have had me watched; two, will have planted evidence to incriminate me. I must know who was watching, to whom he will report, and the nature and the whereabouts of the evidence. You understand?'

I understood only too well, and I felt sorry for him. He was bright enough to have spotted the whole set up from the moment he walked into the room at Kotelnicheskaya Street and heard my English voice. He had known he was going to be framed and he had acted quickly. By having me picked up immediately he might have been able to neutralise the whole bit before the trap snapped shut on him. To do this, he had only to learn phase two in my operation and he would be able to clear himself before he was even under suspicion. Unfortunately for him, that's where he hit the snag. I couldn't tell him about phase two, because I didn't know what it was myself. The funny part about it was that he believed me. And, having accepted this fact, he grew mournfully conversational.

'We are tools, you and I,' he said. 'We are like the stone, the scissors and the paper in that stupid game. Stone blunts scissors, scissors cut paper, paper wraps stone. The unfortunate thing for us is that we don't know which we are. In this case, you are the scissors and I am the paper. It could have been the other way round.'

I was following him admirably and, in some places, I was way ahead of him. What he didn't know was that while I was scissors to his paper, there was a bloody great rock to my scissors waiting in the background ready to blunt me to hell and gone. But knowing it wasn't going to help him any, so I kept quiet.

The conversation moved on. He had already accepted that he was dead and buried as far as his professional life was concerned and he grew comparatively loquacious. This meant that he assumed that I was dead and buried alongside of him. Although he was going to get the sharp edge of the chopper from his employers, he was still sufficiently professional not to give away any secrets unless he was dead sure the giving away would harm no one.

He told me a great many things that I didn't know. And it wasn't because I had been out of the Service for six years; these were things that I was sure Max himself was unaware of. Normally I would have been both interested and fascinated by some of his disclosures, but all I could see now was that each new revelation was just another nail in my coffin.

After half an hour he had a bottle of vodka sent in and we killed it together, drinking solemn toasts to one another. I wasn't aware of the fact at the time, but I suppose I should have been grateful that he didn't stick bamboo splinters under my fingernails or red hot pokers up my ass. In similar circumstances, had our positions been reversed, I am not at all sure that I would not have descended to such vulgarities, especially had my entire life been hanging in the balance, as his was. For the next ninety minutes we grew steadily more drunk and our conversation veered from the professional to the sentimental.

He told me all about his girl friend, the one whose name had been used to involve him. I told him all about Anne Ballard, assuming that the telling could do no harm whatsoever; which only goes to prove how wrong you can be when there is half a bottle of vodka slopping around inside your stomach.

But the crunch had to come eventually. After two hours Vladimir suddenly pricked up his ears at some sounds in the corridor outside. To me they were just sounds, like all the others we had been hearing since we had been closeted together. But Vladimir knew different. He rose to his feet dramatically. He raised his glass and toasted me once more, this time in Russian. Then, like something straight out of Tolstoy, he flung the glass over his shoulder where it shattered on the wall behind him. Feeling that something was required of me, I, too, rose to my feet and lifted my glass, which was unfortunately empty, and intoned *my* farewell toast.

'Mud in your eye,' I said.

I upended the empty glass and, with an equally grandiloquent gesture, I flung it backwards over my shoulder. Unfortunately I was standing with my back to the door, which was opened from the outside as my glass flew over my shoulder and shattered, inches away from the head of a thin, hawk-faced individual who was just entering. Not surprisingly, one of the uniformed men who had accompanied him, and who were standing outside the door, scrabbled for his revolver, assuming no doubt I was making a desperate attempt to escape. Vladimir shouted something in Russian and Hawkface repeated it. The uniformed man subsided, looking disappointed.

There followed a staccato exchange in Russian between Vladimir and Hawkface. Vladimir was obviously getting the worst of this interchange, but he went down with all flags flying. After half a dozen rapid sentences, he drew himself up to attention, bowed stiffly towards Hawkface, turned, bowed towards me and walked out of the room with his head held high. I would have liked to have told him that everything would be all right, but I didn't believe for one moment that it would. So I kept quiet and, when Hawkface indicated that I should precede him out of the room, I also drew myself up to attention, executed a stiff little bow, and did as he asked, crunching my way across a pile of shattered glass.

I had thought Vladimir and his men were efficient, but Hawkface and his crowd soon put them to shame. I was out of the building and in the back of a car before I could catch my breath. At our destination I was whisked out of the car and into a building so quickly that it was impossible for me to take in any of my surroundings. It wasn't until much later that I discovered that I was actually inside the walls of the Kremlin.

I was rushed down two or three anonymous corridors so fast that my feet barely touched the ground and was finally deposited in a cell. It wasn't bad as cells go; there was a reasonable looking bed, a table, a chair and a flush toilet lurking behind an inadequate screen in one corner. But it was a cell nevertheless, and I am of the opinion that even if one got David Hicks to design the interior, a cell will always be a cell. There are bars on the windows and a lock on the door; these have a psychological effect that no amount of flim-flam or chintz can disguise.

It was only after the door had been slammed shut behind me that I realised that nobody had spoken a single word to me since Vladimir had made his dignified departure. This could have been merely anti-social but was more likely due to the fact that from here on in my every utterance was to be recorded for posterity. They, with a capital T, didn't want my words wasted on the hired help. Hawkface I now relegated to this category. It was going to be interesting to see how high up the KGB ladder They considered they should climb before they reached an interrogator worthy of my importance.

*　　*　　*

Somewhere in the Manual, it says that a suspect should be left alone for at least five hours before interrogation commences. This is designed to put the fear of God into the suspect, undermining his confidence and giving him serious doubts as to what his eventual fate will be. Either the Russians did not use the same manual or they considered my confidence was already undermined to a degree where further waiting would be superfluous. In this, they were right. The last vestiges of my confidence, courage, or what-have-you had leaked out of me back there in Kotelnicheskaya Street.

I hardly had time to use the toilet and ascertain that the plumbing was not as efficient as it looked, when the door was opened again. Two uniformed men stood outside and one of them barked something at me in Russian. I suppose I must have looked unco-operative, standing there doing up my flies, because a moment later the two of them came into the cell, grabbed an arm each, and hustled me out through the door.

I was taken to a large, well lit, efficient looking room, where I was fingerprinted and photographed before being escorted to a smaller room which was furnished even worse than my cell. There were a table and two upright wooden chairs, and I had been in the trade long enough to know that this was where we got down to business. There were no windows and the walls were tiled to a height of six feet. The floor, too, was tiled and very slightly funnelled to a soakaway drain set in the centre of the room. There was a water tap bolted to one of the walls, with a short length of hose fixed to it. They had obviously removed the thumb screws and the rack for the time being, but their message was there for all who had eyes to see. I was shoved hard into one of the chairs and a moment later the two uniformed men snapped to attention as Comrade-Colonel Nicolas Borensko came into the room.

I have a reasonably good memory for faces; but, more important, it is a selective memory. This means that I can recall the important faces that crop up now and again, without having the filing system cluttered up with the unimportant ones. This one was a very important face. I had never seen it in the flesh before, but in the old days Max had kept a file in which there were photographs and details of the dozen or so men he would most have liked to get his hands on. Even after six years I recognised Borensko from the top of Max's file. This wasn't as difficult as it sounds, because Borensko had just about the ugliest scar I have ever seen. It started somewhere near his left temple, pulling back the skin of his eye socket to such an extent that it was a wonder he was ever able to close his eye; it meandered down across his cheek bone, clipped the corner of his mouth and trailed off under his chin down into the collar of his tunic. It was a revolting looking scar and he could easily have had it corrected by plastic surgery. But in his job he had discovered that the mere sight of it gave him such a psychological advantage that he even refused to grow a beard to cover it up.

He was supposed to have come by his disfigurement during the revolution when a White Russian officer had sliced open his face with a sabre. But, if appearances were anything to go by, he didn't look old enough to have been involved in the Revolution and it was generally agreed by people whose job it was to know such things that his face had been opened up with a broken bottle wielded by an irate whore when he had been stationed in Macao early in his career.

He came around the table and sat down in the other chair. He examined the top of the table for a minute and then, seemingly satisfied with it, he shifted his gaze to me. This was extremely off-putting, as no doubt it was intended to be. The whore's bottle or the Czarist sabre had done its work extremely well. In addition to disfiguring him, it had somehow severed some of the muscles that controlled the movement of the eyeball so that his left eye swung free within its socket. I have seen plenty of wandering eyes in my time, but Borensko's really travelled. It flopped about in its socket, darting hither and thither as though it were trying to escape. But, frightening as it was, it was soon forgotten when you looked into his good eye. That one was like a piece of chiselled quartz, muddy grey in colour, and far more intimidating that its wildly erratic companion, the scar, the interrogation room, the KGB or the entire bloody Kremlin.

'Mr King,' he said. I tried to look intelligent. 'You are Mr King?'

I nodded.

'Mr Harrison King?'

I nodded again. Then I did the standard indignant bit which I felt was expected of me. 'I don't know what this is all about,' I said. 'But I want to see the British Consul.'

'No doubt,' said Borensko. 'But I feel the British Consul would not want to see you. No doubt you would be a considerable embarrassment to him.'

I blustered my way through a couple more indignant phrases and then subsided into silence.

'Have you quite finished,' he said. I nodded. 'Good. Then we can get down to business.' he said. 'First, your reason please for being in Moscow at this time?'

'I'm with a trade mission,' I said. 'I sell tractors.'

'I'm not interested in your cover,' he said. 'Only in the purpose of your visit.'

'Tractors,' I said.

He smoothed the surface of the table with his stubby, well kept hands. 'Mr King,' he said. 'I must assume that you are not a fool or you would not be here. Would you please do me the courtesy of assuming the same as far as I am concerned. Now please, your business with Vladimir Karkov?'

'Who?'

He gave me one more chance. 'Your business with Vladimir Karkov?'

'I don't know anyone by that . . .' Anything further I had to say was superfluous. One of the men standing behind me fetched me a clout on the side of the head which lifted me clear out of the chair and deposited me against the wall seven feet away. There was a high-pitched singing in my ear as I was dragged to my feet and dropped back into the chair.

'Your business with Vladimir Karkov?'

I decided about here that enough was as good as a feast and, if I wanted to end the day with my head still on my shoulders, now was the time to start talking.

'I was told to contact him,' I said.

'Told by whom?'

'A man I met in London,' I said. 'I'd never met him before. He gave me five hundred pounds and said I was to contact this man at an address he gave me, and take from him whatever he had to offer, and fetch it back to London.'

'All this for five hundred pounds?' said Borensko.

'I'd cut my own throat for five hundred pounds,' I said.

His good eye regarded me bleakly for a moment. 'I think you have,' he said. He allowed me a few seconds to digest this remark before he continued. 'However, if you are telling the truth, and if you continue to co-operate, perhaps we can salvage something from the wreckage.'

By 'wreckage', I assumed he was referring to me personally.

'I'll be only too happy to co-operate,' I said.

'Please,' he said. 'The name of the man in London?'

'What man?' I said, courting another thump on the head. But I needed time right now. Borensko was not supposed to enquire too deeply into my association with Karkov. The whole Vladimir bit had been designed as a side issue, having no real bearing on the purpose of my visit. And until such time as they were able to compare my fingerprints and photograph with the file on John Smith that must have been somewhere in their archives, I was forced to continue playing the role of the innocent victim of circumstance. I sincerely hoped that their records department was as efficient as their strong arm boys. You can flannel some people for a fair amount of time; a man like Borensko, with luck, you could flannel for ten seconds dead. But somehow over the years, it seems I had lost my knack. I didn't even get ten seconds.

While I was still making up my mind how long I could stretch the current trend of the conversation, he spotted me for the phoney that I was. When interrogation is your business, and you are a master at the job, you can read signs in your subject, without the subject even being aware that he has made any. To this day I don't know what the sign was that gave me away to Borensko, but whatever it was I was grateful for it. There was bound to be a certain amount of table thumping, and even a modicum of John Smith thumping, but at least I would now be getting on to ground that had been partially prepared for me back at the Farm.

He announced the fact that I had not fooled him by suddenly slamming his hand flat down on the table.

'We are wasting time,' he said. 'You are not Harrison King, tractor salesman.'

'Oh,' I said. 'Who am I?'

'I don't know who you are,' he said. 'Just who you are not. And you are not who you would have me believe. Perhaps our records will turn up something.'

As far as I was concerned the pressure was now off, even if only temporarily, and the record department could take as long as they wanted. I wasn't going anywhere. But in the meantime Borensko decided to try to short circuit his filing system and gather his own information. 'If you are not a tractor salesman, then you can only be one other thing; a professional agent. And, if you are a professional agent, then there is more to the Vladimir Karkov affair than you or your employers would have us believe.'

In fact there was considerably less to the Vladimir Karkov affair, but it turned out that this was what he meant anyway.

'A professional agent,' he continued, 'would never contact a man like Karkov in the manner that you did unless he had a special reason. In your case, I believe that the reason was discovery. It was intended that we here should know about your meeting with Karkov. He should be grateful to you. While knowing that he was a good man, we were not aware that he had attained such importance in the eyes of the West. The despatch of an agent to Moscow, purely for the purpose of discrediting him, makes him a very important man indeed.'

He was right; Vladimir had considerable cause for gratitude. Five minutes ago he had been as good as bound for the salt mines. Now it looked as though he was in line for rapid promotion. But we were still on unsafe ground. Borensko had accepted the fact that I was not King, tractor salesman, and that I *was* a professional agent, but he still believed that my sole purpose in visiting Moscow was to discredit Vladimir.

But records didn't let me down. There was a discreet tap on the door, which was answered by one of the uniformed men who had been standing behind me, and a file was handed over and then placed on the table in front of Borensko.

In happier circumstances I would have been extremely flattered. The file was more than two inches thick. Considering I had not worked for the Service for six years, it was a pretty impressive indication as to how effective I had been during my earlier career. As the file was placed in front of him, Borensko looked at me bleakly for a second before examining it. I think he, too, was impressed with the size of the file, but it was impossible to read anything in the flat grey of his single eye. It was remarkable how quickly one forgot its roving companion. It was still wandering around like a lost soul within its strict orbit, but I hardly noticed it at all.

He bent over the file and there was silence for the next ten minutes. The only sound to break the monotony was the occasional rustle of paper as he passed from one document to another. Once he flashed a look at me and I would have liked to have known what he had just read that caused this deviation. Perhaps it had been that fiasco in Algiers, the one that had led

me to quit the Service; then again, it might have been a
report on my part in the crippling of Gustav Heidecker, who
we all understood had been no end of the bright-eyed boy
under the Stalin regime. But whatever it was, he didn't let on.
He continued to shuffle through the file until he gently closed
it up. Then, resting his hands palms down on the blank cover,
he stared at them for a full minute and a half.

Finally he looked up at me once more. 'Mr Smith,' he said,
'There seems to have been a slight inefficiency in our records
department. The last entry on your activities is dated two
years ago and before that another four years. Tell me, please,
where have you been during all this time?'

'Retired,' I said.

'But you are still working,' he said. 'You are here now.'

'I'm staging a comeback.'

He was pleased with himself; there was no doubt of it. His
eye wasn't actually twinkling, but at least it had begun to look
as though it had some sort of life in it. I could understand his
satisfaction and a moment later he confirmed it for me.

'We thought we had caught a little fish. It seems we have
caught a very large one.'

'Not that large,' I said.

'Come, come!' he said. 'You have an impressive record. Do
you realise that at one time you were number three on our list
of most wanted enemy agents?'

I hadn't realised it, but I wasn't going to let him know.
'That was a long time ago,' I said.

He flicked through the file once more, then stopped halfway.
'You shot Leo Tamir,' he said.

There didn't seem much point in denying it. I nodded.

'It's a pity you weren't on your true form that night,' he said.

That made two of us who felt the same way about Leo. I shrugged. 'We all have our off days,' I said.

'Much trouble would have been averted,' he said, as he leafed further through the file. 'There is a flattering report on you by Berat, the Albanian,' he went on, picking on another sheet of paper.

'I didn't know you were still chummy with the Chinese.'

'We're not. This is two years ago.'

'We got on quite well, all things considered,' I said. We had, too, considering we were on opposite sides of the wall.

'And since then you say you have been in retirement?' I nodded. 'You don't expect me to believe you?' he said.

'You might as well. It's true.'

'And the purpose of your present visit?' he said, coming to the crunch.

'Karkov?' I asked.

He shook his head. 'No. Karkov was a side issue, I think. A sort of bonus.' And having hit that nail right on the head he proceeded to bash away some more, his aim becoming even more accurate. 'Let us assume your main purpose in coming here was not to discredit Karkov,' he said. 'It follows that you must have had another reason. And yet you still kept this foolish rendezvous knowing that it was bound to lead to your eventual capture.' His good eye regarded me steadily as though he had asked me a question and was expecting a reply. But he hadn't and he wasn't. 'It's an interesting situation,' he went on. Looking at it from his side of the desk, I suppose it was. 'Of course, there is only one set of conclusions we can draw. Right?' This time he *was* asking a question.

'You tell me,' I said.

'You wished to be captured. It's the object of your visit here. The whole object.'

I said nothing. He was doing very well, thank you, all on his own, and Max's plan was running downhill fast. For if Borensko even began to guess that I had been planted for an exchange, then there wouldn't be one. If Max had been the only consideration I would have chucked the towel in there and then, and a pox on his grandiose scheme. But there was a far more important aspect which had started to hammer around in my head. With no exchange, I had bought a one way ticket to the salt mines. So right here, I started to get busy.

'Of course I didn't intend to be caught,' I said. 'What do you take me for? Some kind of a nut? You've got my file there. That's the file of a man who knows what he's doing because he's done it all before. It's the file of a professional, not a half-assed amateur.'

'So?' he said.

'So you want to know why I'm here, I'll tell you. But you'd better get a stenographer in here, because I'm only saying it once.'

My goodness, I was brave! Nobody talked to Nicolas Borensko that way. But self-preservation is about the only strong basic emotion I can lay claim to and, when it comes to the fore, discretion takes a back seat. And anyway my file showed that I was a tough experienced customer, so I decided that I'd better start acting like one. Because if he truly started to believe that I was a hard up ex-agent, long retired, then I was dead and buried already.

He jabbered something to one of the soldiers behind me and, while the soldier trotted off to find a stenographer, we sat and looked at one another. It didn't seem the time for small talk so, while attempting to look casual and completely at ease, I desperately tried to marshal my thoughts into a semblance of what I hoped he would take for credibility.

The stenographer arrived, a prematurely bald man with thick glasses. He brought his own chair with him and we all watched him while he made himself comfortable.

'First you will tell me in your own words,' said Borensko. 'Then later I will ask you questions.'

I looked towards the stenographer, who nodded, and I was away.

I trotted out all my recently learned information, adding a little here, missing out a little there. I embroidered parts of it and other parts I just sketched in. The important thing at this stage was to leave enough room for enlargement at some later date. The names I trotted out from time to time were just names as far as I was concerned. They may have had people attached to them; I just didn't know. Nor did I much care. They were the names that had been given to me to use, so I used them like there was no tomorrow. If these names, or the material I was spewing forth, meant anything to Borensko, he didn't show it. He just sat there, the only movement coming from his duff eye. If it hadn't been for that, rolling around in its fixed orbit, he could have been dead and embalmed.

I talked for two solid hours, while the stenographer wore out six pencils and filled two notebooks. The soldiers behind me grew bored some way through the proceedings and started to shuffle their feet occasionally. I was being so bloody co-operative that I was surprised Borensko didn't send them off to supper or some such. But he didn't, and for two hours there were just the five of us, with me making all the noise. Then, when I started to get tired, I stopped. There was a long silence during which the stenographer kept his pencil poised. When he realised I had finished he lowered his pencil and closed his notebook quietly. The silence stretched and finally Borensko called an end to the proceedings. He said something to the man behind me and I felt a tap on my shoulder. I got to my feet.

'Thank you Mr Smith,' he said. 'We will talk later.'

'Any time,' I said, generously.

*   *   *

Two minutes later I was in my cell once more and, three minutes after that, I was sound asleep. There were dreams, of course, a huge conglomeration of all that had happened to me in the past twenty-four hours, mixed up so that they made no sense whatsoever. But even awake it didn't make much sense either, especially when viewed from the standpoint that I had walked into the situation with my eyes wide open. However, I slept, and while I slept Borensko put the wheels in motion.

The names I had trotted out so casually were checked and run to ground. The facts were examined, re-examined, and noted upon. A line was opened up to London where a check was made on my movements prior to leaving for Russia. Max had already made provision for this and I passed with flying colours. Everything possible was checked against my statement, then re-checked and verified. My personal effects at the hotel were dissected and disembowelled. No doubt all sorts of goodies came to light there, especially as Max's people had done my packing.

*   *   *

And while all this was going on, I slept for twelve hours, until Borensko called for me again.

'You are in grave trouble, Mr Smith.'

'I know it.'

We were alone this time. The same room, but without the guards. My typed statement lay on the table in front of him and I could see where he had scribbled notes in the margins.

'Very grave trouble,' he said, as though the point needed emphasis. 'But there are aspects here which I do not understand. We will now examine some of them.'

That was the first session. It continued for three hours. Then there was a break of a couple of hours, and we started again.

*   *   *

About here I started to realise that Max hadn't chosen me for this assignment because he liked the colour of my eyes, or even because he thought I could do with the money. He had chosen me because for five years I had been out of the business. Consequently, anything about the internal workings of the Service that I inadvertently gave away was so out of date as to be harmless. And yet I was still steeped in sufficient genuine background material to keep Borensko interested. If it hadn't been for me, I don't think Max would have even contemplated the scheme, I was so damned right for it. At the back of my mind I started cursing the fact that I hadn't asked for more money. But I wasn't in any position to go back and ask for a raise now. So session after session followed with Borensko probing deeper and deeper, until I started to get seriously worried.

Then, just as I was about to run out of answers, it was all over. On the fourth day, as I was getting ready for my morning session in the interrogation room, the door of my cell opened and in came a man I hadn't seen before.

He was neatly and, for a Russian, almost elegantly dressed.

His hair was cut short and he wore a pair of rimless spectacles. When he spoke, it was slowly, as though he was carefully examining each word in this foreign tongue before allowing it into circulation.

'My name is Chenkov,' he said. 'Boris Chenkov.'

He held out his hand and, because it seemed expected of me, I shook it. His handclasp was dry and not very firm. It was as though he would have had a good solid handshake had his heart been in it. In fact, his whole attitude was that of a man whose natural inclination was to be friendly, but whose inbuilt caution slowed him up a little. This turned out to be the situation exactly, as he explained in his next sentence.

'I have been appointed by the State as your defence council,' he said.

I felt like offering him my sympathy. Instead, I smiled and asked him to sit down. He did so, taking the only chair. I sat on the bed, facing him. 'What happens now?' I asked.

'Your trial is set for a week today,' he said. 'We do not have much time to prepare a defence.'

We could have had ten years and it wouldn't have made any difference. I hinted this to him delicately, not wanting to discourage him this early in the proceedings. 'I've signed a statement,' I said.

He looked away from me quickly, then back again. He was actually embarrassed. 'My task will be to persuade the court to reduce your sentence as far as it is possible. As you point out, guilt or innocence are not in dispute.'

'Reduce it from what to what?'

'The death penalty will be demanded,' he said. 'I shall endeavour to get it reduced to life imprisonment.'

'Bully for you!' I said irreverently. I was feeling choked. I didn't know what it was Max had set me up for, but it must have been a beaut for them to have been talking about the death penalty. What price Max's exchange if I was in a box, I thought, and I turned back to friend Chenkov, who was looking a little upset. 'I'm sorry Mr Chenkov,' I said. 'I know you'll do your best.'

He smiled very slightly. 'If I succeed,' he said, 'then things may not be as black as they now seem. Perhaps sometime in the future an exchange will be made.'

Hello, I thought, the plot thickens. I tried to see if there was anything lurking behind the smile, but there didn't seem to be. On reflection, it was a perfectly natural assumption of his; exchanges were the lifeblood of the trade. That's why I was here. I returned his smile.

'What can I do to help you?' I enquired.

It seemed there wasn't much. I should express remorse and shame in equal proportions; I should throw myself on the mercy of the court; I should confess to my errors and to my conversion to the Russian point of view, delivering a hefty thump to the capitalist warmongers in the process. It all added up to my saying that I had been a bad, bad boy and, if you don't spank me too hard, I promise not to do it again.

None of this would, of course, be believed by anyone, East or West, but the whole bit had become formalised in procedure like a badly staged farce. He then asked me if there was anything I wanted and I told him I could do with some decent toilet paper. He promised to speak to a friend at the American Embassy.

'A new toothbrush and some soap,' I added. He made a note in a small black notebook which he took from his jacket pocket.

'And some cigarettes,' I said, beginning to warm up. 'And

matches, of course; some paper and pen and ink; a couple of books – murder stories; an English newspaper or two; a copy of *Time* magazine would be handy, and I could do with a new mattress. The one I've got . . .' He stopped me by snapping shut his notebook. It was a decisive movement, one which signalled that I had overstepped the mark somewhat. He still looked apologetic as he stood up, but there was no sign of it in his voice.

'Please bear in mind, Mr Smith, that you are in prison charged with a capital offence. This is not a holiday resort on the Black Sea.'

'Sorry,' I said.

He smiled once more. 'I shall come and see you again to-morrow and we shall start to prepare the statement you will read out in court.'

He shook my hand again, a little harder this time, and off he went.

Me, I went to bed. There wasn't anything else to do in the cell and exercise appeared to be a dirty word as far as my gaolers were concerned. So I climbed into the sack, pulled the blanket over my head and curled up as tight as I could, wishing I could return to some sympathetic womb.

CHAPTER FIVE

THE TRIAL was a full, showcase affair; foreign press, diplomats, the lot. There hadn't been such a show of righteous indignation since the U2 business. It continued for three days of rock bottom boredom as far as I was concerned. They had provided me with earphones through which the flat voice of the interpreter droned on and on. But, as I knew practically verbatim the course the trial was going to take, it only served to enhance the boredom and after the first couple of hours, I realised that if I had to listen to this voice for the next three days, I would be a basket case. So when no one was looking, I managed to rip out the wires built into the phones. Wearing them after that effectively blotted out what was actually being spoken in the courtroom, so I was spared both the Russian and the English versions.

Occasionally I would see in the courtroom a face I knew, but not often. Neither Vladimir Karkov nor Borensko appeared. As undercover men it was necessary for them to remain undercover. There was an attractive-looking bird who, I later learned, was from the British Embassy, and I spent most of the trial staring at her and indulging in lewd flights of fancy. She must have been able to read the outer edges of my mind because, after the first couple of hours, she started to blush and pull her skirt down round her knees. After that she wouldn't catch my eye again.

I was driven to the courtroom each morning, escorted by three men, and driven back to my cell each evening. My clothes were taken from me when I went to bed and returned, laundered and pressed, before setting out the next day. I was shaved each morning by a vast sergeant who didn't speak a word and who wielded a cut-throat razor like he was decapitating an entire Cossack division. The food improved somewhat and I was even given half a bottle of Russian wine with my dinner.

The case against me, as presented by the Russians, was extremely lucid and beautifully documented. I had come to Moscow disguised as a tractor salesman and had then proceeded to contact various subversives who somehow still managed to exist in Russia. I had offered them money in an attempt to set up some sort of network which was to be used to feed back classified information. The whole thing was straight out of James Bond and far too infantile to fool any but the most gullible. But the Russians were fooled, or so it seemed, which only goes to prove something.

The evidence against me mounted slowly and methodically until even I began to wonder if I hadn't overplayed my hand somewhere along the line. If everything they were saying about me was true, I was too valuable to swap for a brace of Pontecorvos with a Fuchs and a Blake thrown in for good measure. But there was nothing I could do about it except sit and wait.

Comrad-Lawyer Chenkov did his best, but his heart wasn't in it. He pleaded a reasonable case based first on the premise that I wasn't the man everyone thought I was and, when that obviously died the death, he subtly switched tactics and presented me as an ignorant tool of the capitalist system. Here, he fared a little better, and on the fourth day of the trial, with me standing in the dock and looking suitably penitent, I heard the verdict: *Guilty on all counts. Sentenced to fifteen years' hard labour.*

*   *   *

That evening in my cell there was no wine and the dinner was diabolical. I felt as low as it was possible to be which, considering how low I had felt for the past couple of weeks, was pretty abysmal. The attitude of my guards had changed too. While not exactly thumping me, they gave every indication that they would like nothing better, and they gave me the impression they were just begging for an opportunity. So I was good – so good it hurt. I did everything I was told, when I was told. I didn't answer back and I kept myself strictly to myself. Mysteriously, my flush toilet went on the blink and, when I mentioned it apologetically, I was handed a bucket.

*   *   *

After the morning exercise period I lay on my bed and tried to analyse the reason I felt at rock bottom. Discounting the petty inconveniences, none of which really amounted to much, I should have been laughing. The whole plan was working exactly the way Max had predicted it would. All that remained now was for the wheels of international commerce, espionage division, to start grinding and, before you could say Kim Philby, I'd be a free man. A *rich* free man at that – and my mind started to slip sideways to visions of Anne Ballard, Mary and the girl from the British Embassy I had seen in court, and the first girl I had ever laid and the twenty-first. Just as the whole thing was beginning to become embarrassing and I was wondering what to do with my hands, the cell door opened and I was gestured at by a guard. I picked up my bucket, but another gesture from the guard told me it wasn't mucking out time. It seemed that it was visiting time instead

It was Chenkov. He came into the cell and so good were his manners that he didn't even wrinkle his nose. He sat down on my only chair and smoothed the creases in his trousers.

'I did the best I could, Mr Smith,' he said.

'You did very well,' I lied.

'After all,' he said. 'Fifteen years isn't a lifetime. With time off for good behaviour, you could be back home in ten years.'

'That's a great comfort,' I said. He had performed a thankless chore to the best of his ability and a pat on the back wasn't going to cost me anything.

'I have arranged that you will be transferred to Malensk. It will not be so bad there.'

'What's at Malensk?' I asked.

'It is what you call an open prison. The inmates work on the neighbouring farms. It is healthy work. You will eat well and the time will pass quicker.'

'That's very civil of you,' I said. 'Where is it?'

'It is near Vilyuisk, two hundred miles South of the Arctic Circle.'

'Siberia?'

He nodded. 'But it is not as bleak as people make out. During the summer the snow melts for as long as two months.'

'That must be hard on the farmers,' I said, not really interested. He then launched into a discourse on farming near the snowline which, if I had read about it in the *National Geographic*, I would have found quite interesting. But knowing that I was to be personally involved somehow robbed it of its fascination. Sure, I'd be home in three months, but even three weeks of what Chenkov was describing sounded sufficient to kill me stone dead.

He talked on for half an hour, then he rose to his feet. 'It is unlikely that we shall meet again Mr Smith,' he said. 'If you like, and if it is permitted, I shall write to you occasionally. I shall of course lodge appeals on your behalf every three years for the reduction of your sentence, but I am of the opinion that they will not be granted.'

'By all means write to me,' I said. 'Perhaps they will permit me to write back.'

'I understand that you will be allowed to send and receive one letter every two weeks. Is there anyone at home you wish me to contact?'

I thought briefly of Mary and Anne Ballard. Both would have read of my exploits in the newspapers, so there didn't seem much point. I would like to have assured Miss Roberts that everything was not as black as it obviously looked. But even she would survive for three months, by which time I would be home again, as large as life and twenty times richer.

'There's no one,' I said.

He bowed slightly. I believe he was a bit embarrassed. Between him and Vladimir Karkov, the Russians I had met hadn't been at all bad. I'm not by nature a gregarious person, but I could have made friends with either of them had the situation been different. I shook hands with him and he knocked on the cell door to be let out. Then I had an idea. 'Do the Embassy know where I'm going?' I asked.

'They do. But there is nothing they can do for you.'

'Still,' I said with a smile. 'It's a comfort.'

He returned my smile, a little vaguely. The guard opened the door, and that was the last of Comrade-Lawyer Chenkov.

*　　*　　*

Half an hour later my cell door was opened once more and a young officer I hadn't seen before appeared. He spoke atrocious English, but sufficient for me to ascertain that I had three minutes to gather my personal effects together. My personal effects consisted of a toothbrush, half a roll of toilet paper and a bent comb. He told me I wouldn't be needing the toilet paper, which sounded ominous, and with my toothbrush and comb clutched in my hand, I was marched out of my cell for the last time.

It was cold in the yard. I stood with half a dozen bedraggled looking prisoners, while our names were checked and re-checked on innumerable lists. Then we were signed for by an enormous officer with a great bushy moustache. He barked at his sergeant and we were all bundled into the back of a closed van. During our short ride I kept myself to myself, staring steadfastly at a spot on the wall opposite me. This lot were real criminals, not the sort of company I was used to at all. I may have killed a dozen or so assorted villains in the course of my ex-career, but the men sitting with me in the van were thieves, black marketeers and deviationists; it was downright humiliating to be included with them. And it was an even money bet that none of them spoke English anyway. There were two guards sitting in the rear of the van with us, nursing automatic weapons on their laps. But they were expecting no trouble and were plainly bored with the whole operation. As far as I was concerned, trouble from me was one thing they weren't going to get. Didn't I have my passport out of here?

All that was needed was the stamp of official approval and I'd be on my way.

The van was driven to one of the main line stations and straight on to the platform. We were herded out and into two reserved compartments. The passengers standing around the platform regarded us with a disinterested curiosity. Once in the compartment, the blinds were drawn. I was with three other prisoners and one of the guards, so there was plenty of room. By judicious use of an elbow I managed to corner a window seat on the assumption that once the train started they'd raise the blinds. If we were going to do a 'Doctor Zhivago', and travel clean across Russia, I might as well have something other than my companions to stare at for the next four or five days.

The train remained motionless for the next twenty minutes and then, to the accompaniment of shouting and whistling from outside, it jerked and rumbled its way into motion.

*   *   *

For two whole days I sat on that train. Sure enough, they *did* pull up the blinds soon after we left Moscow but, as far as I was concerned, after an hour they might as well have lowered them again. There was nothing to see except mile after mile of flat farmland, stretching from here to God knows where. One hears of food shortages in Russia, when they rush off to buy wheat and cereals from Canada; all I can say is that they must be terrible farmers. There seemed to be enough farmland out there to feed all of Russia and half of China thrown in for good measure. Occasionally the train would roar past a small village, most of them no more than a collection of half a dozen wooden buildings; and once we slowed down to pass through some sort of industrial complex. But just as it was getting interesting, the officer with the whiskers appeared and barked at the guard to pull down the window blinds. This he did, letting them up an hour later, when we were back to the wide open spaces.

*　　*　　*

I suppose the journey *did* take five days; I never found out. On the evening of the second day there was an unscheduled stop. Through the window I could see a tiny platform, backed by a couple of corrugated iron huts. I was trying to work out where we were when Whiskers put in one of his infrequent appearances and I was beckoned out into the corridor. There Whiskers informed me, through an interpreter, that I was to be taken off the train and returned to Moscow immediately.

I was driven from the station to a small airfield where I was escorted into an army plane. It was a big one, with four jets, and my spirits began to lift somewhat. If someone had considered it worth sending a plane this big, they must have wanted me back in Moscow very badly indeed. I seriously doubted for one moment that the pilot would be able to get it off the ground in the limited space that the airfield offered and, well strapped in, I watched through the window as we gathered speed towards a point where the airstrip ended and the ploughed fields took over. But a couple of seconds before we would have been among the cabbages, there was a great thump, I was slammed back in my seat, and the aircraft seemed to rise vertically, the engine noises drowned out by the roar of the rocket assisted takeoff. Very impressive, I thought, as I was quietly sick into a paper bag.

The journey to Moscow, which had taken two days on the train, took three hours in the plane. We touched down just after midnight and there was a car waiting at the end of the runway. I was bundled into the back with my escort and we were driven to a forbidding looking building somewhere in the centre of the city. There I was handed over with my documents, signed for, and escorted down a mile and a half of corridor. I was steered into a cell, the door was clanged shut behind me, and that seemed to be that.

* * *

At eleven o'clock the following morning, after I'd had a reasonable breakfast, Comrade-Lawyer Chenkov stepped into my life once more. He was all smiles and greeted me as though we hadn't seen each other for God knows how long.

'Mr Smith. How are you? You look fine,' he said, wringing my hand. I mumbled something appropriate and waited for him to get to the meat. I knew what was coming and I prepared to look suitably surprised and grateful.

'You have been brought back to Moscow on the instructions of Comrade-Colonel Borensko,' he said.

'Why?' I asked, slipping easily into my part.

He smiled again, unable to contain himself. 'It is not official of course, but I understand there is the distinct possibility of an exchange being made.'

I widened my eyes in surprise. 'Really?' I said. 'What sort of an exchange?'

He was dying to tell me everything he knew, but discretion took the upper hand. 'I can tell you no more,' he said. 'But no doubt Comrade Borensko will want to see you personally.'

I doubted that. Borensko wouldn't become personally involved in an exchange, any more than Max would. They would both push their respective buttons and the machinery would do the rest. All of which goes to show that I didn't know what I was talking about because, at ten the following morning, I was taken to see Borensko.

Obviously this was 'let's-be-friends' day, because he was wearing an eye patch. It didn't hide his scar, but it blotted out his erratic eye and made him considerably easier to look at. He even got to his feet when I came into the room he was using and, in case there were still lingering doubts that we were pals, he dismissed the guards immediately.

'Sit down Mr Smith,' he said. I sat. 'Cigarette?' He handed me a long brown Russian cigarette and then lit it for me with a lighter that could have been silver, but which I knew was platinum. 'What did Chenkov tell you?' he said when he was sure I was comfortable.

'Nothing,' I said. Then I qualified it. 'Nothing that I fully understood.'

'Then I shall start at the beginning,' he said. He then went on to explain that immediately after my conviction, the lines of communication to London had been opened up and, after careful probing, a meeting had been arranged in East Berlin between one of his men and one of Max's. It seemed that we in England were holding a man whom the Russians wanted back here in the fold, one Gregori Antonov. It also seemed that the English wanted me back where I belonged. So, being civilised human beings, what could be more natural than to arrange an exchange. I did the full Olivier bit, while he was explaining all this, registering surprise, delight and relief, all in equal proportions. When he reached the end of his little dissertation Borensko spread his hands, for all the world like a Russian peasant explaining why he couldn't pay his taxes. 'So you see, Mr Smith, in two or three weeks' time you will be back at home where you belong, and so will Comrade Antonov. Of course, you will give me your personal undertaking that you will never again resume the job that you do so well.' Here he patted my file which was on the table beside him.

'Of course not,' I said.

'No, of course not,' he agreed, convinced I was lying, and convinced that I knew that he knew I was lying. The funny thing was that I was telling the truth. I'd been hooked into this by the short hairs of my own avarice and I had no intention of going anywhere near Max or his kind ever again.

'We on our part,' he said, 'have given your people a similar undertaking with regard to Antonov.'

'Naturally,' I said. The whole thing was a pantomime and we both knew it. But there are formalities that have to be observed, and we observed them meticulously.

'I apologise that you were brought here last night,' he went on. 'Things moved too quickly for me to make proper arrangements for your comfort.'

They hadn't moved so quickly that he wasn't able to organise a bloody great rocket-assisted jet to pick me off a train in the middle of Russia, but I let the matter ride.

'As soon as we have finished here, you will be taken to a place I am sure you will find more agreeable.'

'I could do with a change of clothes,' I said.

'That has all been arranged,' he said, getting to his feet. 'And now I shall say good-bye. It is unlikely that we will meet again.' And here he showed me the gold in his teeth. I think he was smiling. 'I do not think I shall be visiting your country,' he said. 'And I sincerely hope that you will not be visiting mine again.'

I made polite noises, shook his hand, and was escorted out of the room by the same guards who had brought me there. I didn't even return to my cell. I was whipped out through a back door and into a car, which headed out of the city at a rate of knots.

*　　*　　*

Two hours later we pulled on to a side road and the country started to get wooded. Three miles into the trees, we stopped outside an impressive looking pair of gates. They were set into a wall, fifteen feet high, topped with insulated barbed wire. The wall disappeared into the trees without break for about three hundred yards in either direction. There was a guard-room just inside the gates and our papers were carefully checked. Then one of the guards climbed into the front of the car and started directing the driver.

We were in what looked like a large private park. The main drive headed slightly uphill, but after half a mile we turned off this on to a smaller track. A moment later I caught a glimpse through the trees of what lay at the end of the main drive. It was an old house, slightly smaller than Buckingham Palace, but not much. As a relic of Czarist Russia, the Communists could have charged visitors five roubles a head on bank holidays. But ever practical, they had put it to better use. I learned later that the whole place, the house and the grounds, was nothing more than a detention centre. A four star, *de luxe*, Category A type detention centre to be sure, but a prison nevertheless. Here came the V.I.P's; the deposed leaders, while the Party was making up its mind what to do with them; and the foreigners, who had earned detention, but not so conclusively that the Russians weren't sure what sort of fuss the detainee's Government might kick up.

Apart from the main house, there were a number of chalets dotted about among the trees. It was to one of these that I was taken. There I was handed over politely to the man whose job it was going to be to look after me. He was six feet seven inches tall and built like a brick outhouse. He spoke no English and, when he smiled, which he did often, he exposed a set of extremely ill-fitting false teeth. His name, of course, was Ivan and after the first ten minutes, when I was sure he could speak no English, I started to call him Terrible. He pointed out to me in Russian that it was his job to buttle for me and, while he gave every outward indication that his only purpose was to serve, he left no doubts that if I put so much as a foot wrong, he'd cut it off at the knee.

The chalet consisted of a living room, kitchen, bathroom, and two bedrooms. The bedrooms were arranged in such a way that to get to mine, it was necessary to pass through Terrible's. My room was pleasant enough, with a wardrobe, dressing table, double bed and full length curtains; but the curtains were for effect, because there was no window. I also had to go through Terrible's room to get to the bathroom. This didn't disturb me unduly, but the combination of the cold and my unreliable bladder was going to rob Terrible of a lot of sleep.

My suitcase, which I had last seen when I had been dragged out of my hotel, was waiting for me. Terrible helped me unpack and hang up the awful clothes that Max's men had chosen to fit the image of Harrison King, tractor salesman.

After that I sat in front of a roaring fire in the living room, while Terrible sat across from me, examining his fingernails and occasionally grinning broadly in my direction. About four o'clock I heard noises in the kitchen and I glanced towards

Terrible for enlightenment. He called out something and a moment later a pleasantly plain girl came in from the kitchen. She was wearing an apron and looked like domesticity personified. It seemed that she was our non-resident housekeeper. She cooked the meals and did the general chores while Terrible sat on my back, making like a butler-cum-companion, and failing in his attempts not to look like a gaoler.

The girl smiled shyly at me and bobbed a strictly non-Party-line curtsy in my direction. I leered back at her and she returned to the kitchen. A moment later Terrible got to his feet and dragged me over to a cupboard which he opened proudly, showing me that it contained a fair assortment of booze. He made extravagant gestures signifying that I should ask for what I wanted. I pointed to the vodka bottle and, beaming, he poured me three fingers. Three of *his* fingers practically filled a tumbler, but I wasn't driving, so I took it and began to anticipate the delights of getting stoned out of my mind. I pantomimed for him to have one too, but he shook his head emphatically. From the size of him he could have drunk me under seventeen different tables, but he was obviously going to take no chances. But while he wasn't going to drink with me, he was prepared to keep me amused. He dragged out a chessboard and, when I nodded, he happily set out the pieces. I decided that I would show this bumped up yokel that the Russians weren't the only chess players in the world and I started right out to massacre him. Fifteen minutes later he had me tied up so tight that I counted his pieces to make sure he hadn't sneaked a couple of spare queens on to the board when I wasn't looking. He hadn't, and I magnanimously conceded the game to him. He offered to play me again, this time without his queen, but I declined.

I was getting smashed by now; I wasn't talking funny or staggering around the place, but I had begun to entertain lecherous thoughts towards the domestic help. And while one section of my mind indulged in lewd flights of fancy, another kept reminding me that she really was a very plain girl, with a figure like a badly packed laundry sack. Terrible meandered off towards the kitchen – perhaps he wasn't as particular as I was – and with the fire going and a gentle background of voices mumbling in the background, the booze finally gained the upper hand. The next thing I knew was Terrible shaking me awake and pointing me in the direction of the dinner table. It was a good dinner, but I didn't do it justice. All of a sudden the past few weeks seemed to catch up with me. The arrest, the interrogations, the trial, the train journey, the return by plane, the bad food, the cells, the cold and the damp. I must have fallen face forward in my *borscht*, because I was vaguely conscious of being lifted to my feet and propelled towards the bedroom. There Terrible had me out of my clothes and into bed before I knew what was happening. The last thing I remember was his amiable face bending over me as he tucked me in. Then the lights went out and I died for thirty-two straight hours.

*   *   *

A week passed pleasantly enough. Terrible and I would go for walks in the parkland, and occasionally I'd see other members of our little community through the trees, each with his own version of Terrible. But we were never allowed to meet and, on the odd occasions when it looked as though head-on collisions would be unavoidable, my Terrible, or the other man's, always managed a diversion of some sort.

But by the end of the first week the novelty of living like a human being again was beginning to wear a bit thin. There had been no word from Borensko or from anyone else. I was sick of being beaten at chess by Terrible and he didn't know how to play anything else. The half dozen books in the chalet were all in Russian and my requests for something in English fell on stony ground. So, on the morning of the seventh day, I woke up deciding to be ugly. I sulked at breakfast and, when Terrible suggested a walk, I snarled at him with fluent obscenity. But if I hoped to get him annoyed or to hurt his feelings, I was unlucky. He nodded politely as though he understood and went to sit across the room on his own. When I got up to go to the toilet, he followed me as always, and took up his usual position outside the door. I was so bloody bored I even contemplated breaking the mirror and slashing my wrists. Terrible would see that I didn't come to any real harm, and it might have relieved the monotony somewhat. But reason prevailed and all I did was to stay there long enough to worry Terrible sufficiently for him to come in and get me out.

I refused to eat my lunch and was rewarded by a hurt look in the eyes of our cook. But it was during the afternoon that I really came into my own. I started drinking in lieu of lunch, and by four o'clock I was well and truly zonked. Terrible was sitting off in a corner working out a chess problem and, full of booze and pent up irritation, I walked over to him and swept all the pieces off the board.

'What are you going to do about *that?*' I said, looking at the two of him sitting there.

He gazed at me placidly for a moment from all four of his eyes, then he reached down and started to pick up the chessmen, putting them back on the board.

While he was bending forward I emptied my glass down the back of his neck. He jumped to his feet quickly and, in doing so, quite accidentally, he bumped into me. That was it as far as I was concerned. I aimed a swipe at him designed to take his head off, at the same time lining up another blow which I was going to use when he ducked out of the way of the first. But he didn't duck. He just stood there and my first blow, the decapitating one, landed dead on target, just in front of and slightly below his left ear. He made no effort to ride the punch, and it was just like hitting a lump of concrete. I swear he didn't even blink, but I couldn't be too sure of this as I was too busy nursing a hand in which I was willing to bet that every single bone was shattered. Perhaps he thought I hadn't finished, because the next thing he did was to raise a hand, with one finger extended, and poke it into my diaphragm. All co-ordination and control left me suddenly, and he caught me deftly as I collapsed to the floor like a tent that has had all the guy ropes and poles removed at the same time. He carried me into the bedroom and laid me out tidily, where I stayed for the next three hours trying to rebuild myself from scratch.

*　　*　　*

For the next three days I behaved myself. I wasn't affability, but at least I pretended to be civilised. If Terrible bore any grudge, he didn't show it. He was the same, amiable bear of a man he had been before. Only once did he show that my afternoon's stupidity had made any impression on him. That was two days later when I stopped in the woods to have a pee, and for two seconds he didn't realise that I wasn't still with him. When he *did* realise it, he moved incredibly quickly and in a moment he spotted me standing behind a tree poisoning the roots. He relapsed immediately into his ambling self, but he permitted himself a little shake of the head to signify that I shouldn't frighten him like that again; and to add weight to his argument, he held up the finger he had used to demolish me, and waggled it at me like a nanny admonishing a naughty little boy. I waggled back at him, then put myself away and did up my zip.

*   *   *

The fourth day dawned like any other. I was lying in bed on the edge of sleep, wondering what the hell I had to get up for, when Terrible came in and gestured that I was to get dressed. When I showed signs of turning over and going back to sleep, he picked up my bedside clock and with a bit of absurd panto-mime he indicated that a car was coming for me in half an hour. This was it, I thought – the moment of truth, pay day. I was shaved, dressed and packed in twenty minutes, waiting outside when the car arrived. Terrible and his female helper stood on the doorstep to say their good byes. I shook them both by the hand feeling for all the world like a country squire saying good bye to two faithful old retainers.

Then into the car and back to Moscow. I sat comfortably in the back with visions of being home and dry by the end of the week. I expected to be driven straight to one of the better hotels, where I would stay while the final formalities were gone through. I wasn't. I was driven straight back to the gaol I had left ten days earlier.

*   *   *

There didn't seem much point in yelling and screaming at the guards; and, anyway, I was far too frightened. Something had gone seriously wrong somewhere. I sat in my cell chewing my fingernails to shreds and feeling sick, until half an hour later I was hauled out and escorted to an interview room.

Waiting for me was a tall, thin man in a black jacket and pinstripe trousers. There was a bowler hat and an umbrella on the table, beside them a leather briefcase with the legend E II R stamped on it. I was close to panic by now.

'It's about bloody time,' I said, before Pinstripes could open his mouth. 'I've been in and out of gaol for the past five weeks, and you're the first indication I've had that we've even *got* an Embassy in Russia.'

'My name is Beamish,' he said. 'Philip Beamish.'

'I don't give a fuck what your name is,' I said, in full flow now. 'Just tell me why I've been brought back here, then do something about getting me out.'

His left eyelid had started to twitch; whether from anger or embarrassment at what he was about to say, I didn't know. Nor did I care. 'Calm yourself Mr Smith,' he said, trying to keep his voice on an even keel. 'Histrionics will get us no-where.' He glanced at the guard who was minding his own business in the corner of the room. It was important to Beamish to preserve the British image of stiff upper lip and all that nonsense. But my upper lip had lost its starch way back, and I wasn't about to re-stiffen it just so Beamish could keep the Union Jack flying.

'I'll behave any damn way I please,' I stormed. 'Now tell me what's going on before I lose control.'

If he could have cut my throat there and then, he would have done so with pleasure. Instead he sat down and indicated for me to do the same. I did so reluctantly.

'As you know,' he said. 'An exchange was in the process of

being arranged. Yourself for Gregori Antonov.' I nodded, not trusting myself to open my mouth. 'There's been a slight snag,' he went on.

'How slight?'

He cleared his throat. 'Not slight at all as a matter of fact.'

'So tell me,' I said, bracing myself for disaster.

'The snag lies with Antonov himself,' Beamish continued.

I jumped in on him. 'The bastard doesn't want to be exchanged,' I said. 'So tell him to get stuffed and deliver him here anyway.'

'It's not as simple as that,' said Beamish primly.

'It is for me,' I said. 'I want out of here, and friend Antonov is my ticket. Now get moving on it and don't come to me with any more balls about snags. You tell Max he won't know what the word 'snag' means until I get started. And if he doesn't get me out of here in one week flat, I'll open my mouth so wide you'll be able to lose the entire British Embassy in it.'

Beamish had looked horrified when I mentioned Max's name and glanced over his shoulder towards the disinterested guard. Now he turned back to me, tight lipped, livid with anger, and relishing what he was about to say next.

'It will be impossible to arrange an exchange between you and Antonov,' he said. 'Because two days ago Gregori Antonov suffered a heart attack.'

Then, in case the full import of what he was saying had failed to impress me sufficiently, he hammered in the last nail.

'He's dead.'

CHAPTER SIX

HAVING ENTERED my life with such dramatic effect, the British Embassy couldn't wait to get out of it again. Apart from that one traumatic interview with Beamish, I never saw hide nor hair of them again. As far as they were concerned, I was the *persona* most *non grata* in existence. Russian diplomats would drop my name casually when they were arguing delicate points of diplomacy with their British counterparts; while the British tried to pretend I never existed. For while both sides were fully aware that spies and other such villains existed, there was a tacit understanding that the fact was never referred to. But I had upset the *status quo* and committed the unpardonable sin of being caught, with all its attendant publicity. So for a short time the Russians made hay of the fact, and the British wished I would disappear into a large hole.

As for me, it took me twenty-four hours to recover from the shock. Then I started to yell. I yelled so loudly and so consistently that someone *had* to take notice. I wanted to see Borensko and I wanted to see him before they put me back on that bloody train. This time there would be no aeroplane to pluck me from the middle of the Steppes and, if I was going to have to spend the next fifteen years digging up Russian potatoes, I wanted to leave a lot of bleeding corpses behind me. And I wanted Max to be the bloodiest of them all. He'd got me into this impossible situation and I was determined that he was going to suffer for every furrow I had to hoe.

So I yelled. I yelled at the guard who escorted me with my bucket and I yelled at the guard who brought me my food; I yelled at the officers who inspected the cells twice a day, and I yelled at anyone in uniform who I saw in the exercise yard. I tried to get hold of Chenkov to yell at him too, but he never appeared, so after a while I forgot about him and concentrated on trying to get through to Borensko. And somewhere along the line I must have succeeded, because just after lights out on the third day, the guards came to my cell and gave me two minutes to get dressed. I thought for a moment the train had arrived and I started to protest, until one of the guards who had been forced to listen to me for the past three days, jabbed me with the barrel of his sub-machine gun. It wasn't as painful as Terrible's finger, but well on the way. So I got dressed and was escorted along corridors, up stairs, and along more corridors until I suddenly found myself in a room with Borensko. My immediate relief evaporated somewhat when I realised that it was an interrogation room and he wasn't wearing his eye patch. He was sitting behind the table, looking one part bored and three parts angry.

'You have been making a great deal of fuss, Mr Smith,' he said.

'I wanted to see you.'

'If it wasn't for the fact that I don't like my name shouted around the place, I would have left you to rot.'

'That's why I shouted it.'

'I could also have had you silenced.'

'You couldn't do that,' I said. 'I'm a much publicised, well documented prisoner.'

134

'So what have you to say to me?'

'I want to go home,' I said, trying to keep my lower lip from trembling.

'No doubt,' he said. 'And with time off for good behaviour, you will probably be released in ten years.'

'I want to go home now. And I want you to send me home.'

His good eye stared at me unblinking. The less said about the other, the better. He digested my remark well, before answering. 'What reason would I have for sending you home?'

'You'll think of something,' I said.

This time the silence was longer.

'You are offering me some sort of a bargain?' he asked finally.

'I made a bargain with Max that backfired,' I said. 'Perhaps I can make one with you that won't.'

'What bargain did you make with Max?'

So I told him the lot. Before I was halfway through, he was on the phone. Having found out that their prize man in the U.K. was working for the home team, there were a lot of re-adjustments to be made, and quickly. Between calls he prompted me to continue. Finally it was all over, and he relaxed slightly. 'Gregori Antonov did us a great favour by dying,' he said.

'He didn't do me much good though.'

'True.'

'So?' I said, wondering whether I'd lost him for ever.

'So now you want to work for us?'

'Not in any permanent capacity,' I said. 'Just one job that will buy me my ticket home.'

'For example?'

I shrugged. In for a penny, I thought. 'You want someone killed perhaps?' I said, not too hopefully.

He shook his head. 'No, Mr Smith. I have executioners for that sort of work.'

'Men like Leo Tamir,' I said, merely stating a fact, but as it turned out unconsciously turning the key in the door marked Exit.

'Yes,' he said. 'Men like Leo Tamir.' And as he said it, his one good eye suddenly got itself a withdrawn expression. What the other eye was doing was anybody's guess. Me, I was busy looking at his good eye and wondering whether I'd hit a jackpot without knowing it. 'If I remember rightly, you tried to kill Leo Tamir once.'

'A long time ago,' I said, starting to feel my way.

'He was no good to us after that. We should have let him die.'

'You should indeed,' I said, starting to feel solid ground under my feet.

'We've lost track of him,' said Borensko.

'He's working for the CIA,' I said.

Borensko dismissed the fact with a wave of his hand. 'We know that,' he said. 'What we *don't* know is where, and at what.'

'He was in England five weeks ago,' I said. 'He briefed me on part of this job.'

'Is he still there?'

'Could be,' I said. 'If he isn't, he could be got.'

'How?'

'Something could be arranged,' I said.

'Could it really, Mr Smith?' He was asking me a direct question now, and on the answer hung fifteen years of my life.

'Definitely,' I said, without hesitation.

He was nibbling at the bait. I tried to think of something that would make him bite hard. 'I might say I could almost guarantee it,' I said after a moment. He still said nothing and I could practically hear the wheels in his head clicking over, sorting out the various permutations and complications of what I was offering. It would be a big feather in his cap. Not only would he be bringing back a defector for retribution but he'd be getting a window into the workings of the CIA. After all, Leo Tamir had been working for them for a long time now and he must have packed away a pretty useful store of information in that time. I didn't doubt for a moment that Borensko would be perfectly capable of extracting every ounce of it before Leo finally succumbed. He had closed his good eye while digesting all this. The other one continued to revolve erratically. I waited for the good one to appear again; therein lay the key. He reopened it finally.

'I will think about it,' he said. I'd have liked something a little more concrete, but there was no point in pushing my luck any further than I already had. I got to my feet. 'Take your time, Colonel. I'm not going anywhere.'

He smiled. At least, I think it was a smile. 'No, you're not,' he said.

And that was the end of the interview.

*   *   *

The following day a draft left the prison bound for the long train ride to the wide open spaces. And I wasn't included, which made my day. I'd thought that Borensko would have had the good manners to change my accommodation, seeing that we were now on the same side, and I even began to look forward to seeing Terrible again. But nothing happened in that direction and when I was sent for, seven days later, I was still languishing in the same cell.

They came for me at eight o'clock in the evening and I was taken to a dressing room where I was told to change and to bring my overcoat with me. Then I was escorted out into the prison yard to a large black car. Borensko was waiting for me in the back of the car. He was out of uniform and wearing an eye patch, which was encouraging. He said 'Good evening' to me politely enough, and that was all.

We had been driving for ten minutes before I got curious enough to open my mouth.

'Where are we going?'

'To the theatre,' he said flatly.

Ask a silly question, I thought. But to the theatre we went. We pulled up outside a small theatre fifteen minutes from the centre of the city. Once inside the foyer we were hurried up-stairs by a man I assumed was the manager, and through a door into a box. The show was already in progress and the theatre was full; the Russians will go and see anything, and what they were seeing at the moment was an acrobatic act composed of two men and a girl. It was pretty diabolical, as acts go, but the audience seemed to like it. I was too busy wondering what I was doing here to pay much attention, until one of the men in the act, stepping forward to take his bow, distinctly said: 'Thank you, ladies and gentlemen.' And he said it in English. I glanced sideways at Borensko, but he was watching the stage and didn't or wouldn't catch my eye. But I knew what was going to happen and I started to feel sick.

Sure enough, the acrobats finished, the lights dimmed and when they came up again a piano had been wheeled on to the stage. Two seconds later, there was Anne Ballard, looking like a million roubles, and twice as beddable as when I last saw her.

She still spoke her songs rather than sang them, and the effect was still the same, sexy virginity. The audience may not have been able to understand the lyrics but they loved her anyway. Me, I just started to curse fluently under my breath and, if I'd had a knife handy, I would happily have cut my throat. Because it was me who was to blame, me and my big drunken mouth. A bottle of vodka with Vladimir Karkov, and I had presented them with Anne on a platter.

I found out later that Borensko had moved very fast after our last conversation. A member of the Russian Embassy had called on Harvey Stubbs and asked him to book an entire variety bill for a week in Moscow, followed by a tour of some of the Russian cities. Once Harvey had gotten over the shock, he borrowed two acts from another agent, parcelled them with three of his own clients including of course Anne, who was an integral part of the deal, and four days later, here they were.

Borensko allowed me to sit through all of Anne's act. As she left the stage to loud applause, he stood up. 'Charming,' he said. 'Shall we go?' We went.

*   *   *

'It is perfectly straightforward,' he said to me later that evening. 'Miss Ballard and her companions will be in Russia for five weeks. That means you have five weeks to deliver Leo Tamir to us.'

'How?' I asked.

'That is your problem. It was your idea, remember?'

'And if I don't?' It was a silly question.

'Miss Ballard will remain in Russia.'

'There'll be a fuss.'

'Come Mr Smith.' He was right. There'd be an accident, and exit Anne, clean and simple. I tried to tell myself 'so what?', but I'm a selfish bastard from way back and I knew that it was more than just Anne's future in the balance; my own was there right beside hers. If I didn't produce Leo, not only would Anne go to the wall, but I'd be discovered in some dark alley with my head beaten in with a hammer and my heart cut out with a sickle. When I didn't say anything, he continued: 'You wanted a bargain. Now you have one. A simple case of exchange. Anne Ballard for Leo Tamir.'

'It was a simple case of exchange before,' I said.

He shrugged. 'You must make sure this one doesn't go wrong, mustn't you.'

'Yes, sir,' I said. And that seemed to be that.

*　　*　　*

East Berlin was as depressing as it had always been. And the way over the Wall was just as simple, provided one knew the right people. Borensko had seen to it that I knew the right people, and two hours after landing in East Berlin, I was checking into the Hilton in the Western sector.

My passport said I was a Mr Barnet Wimpole, salesman. I wasn't sure what I was supposed to be selling, but it didn't really matter. The passport was designed to get me out of West Berlin. After that I could use it or not, as the fancy took me. I certainly wasn't going to fly into London Airport. Max always had the odd man hanging around watching arrivals and departures, and I hadn't decided yet when I wanted Max to know that the prodigal had returned. One thing was for sure, when he *did* find out, it was going to be on my terms and not because some eagle eyed flat foot spotted me coming through customs.

I showered and shaved, mutilated half a bottle of vodka, and went out to exercise my urges. You can find anything you want in West Berlin, providing you know where to look. I used to know where to look, but five years had washed an awful lot of people under the bridge. There had been a time when I'd been quite a big wheel in the seamier side of the Berlin social scene. But everyone seemed to have moved, married, or died. Three frustrated hours later, I was back in my hotel room alone. I had been propositioned by a woman who reminded me of my grandmother, and by a beautiful young girl who, on closer examination, proved to be a beautiful young boy.

I asked the hotel switchboard to give me an eight o'clock call and by ten I was on an aeroplane to Paris.

At Orly airport I hired a self-drive car and drove the three hours to Le Touquet. I left the car there, flew British United to Lydd, where I hired another car. Ten minutes later I was on the main road to London, wondering where the hell I was bound for. My own flat was out; that would have been too obvious. Mary seemed a natural choice, but I didn't want to mix her up in the nastiness that was to come. But thoughts of Mary led me to thoughts of Anne, and thoughts of Anne led naturally to The Rabbit Warren. With Anne away, her kid sister would be staying with her aunt, and The Rabbit Warren was about as anonymous a place as I could wish for.

I parked my car at the back of the block and used one of the rear doors. On the sixth floor, I walked along to 625 and rang the bell. Nobody answered the door and, after ringing once again just to be sure, I let myself in with a visiting card. The apartment was exactly as I had last seen it, complete to the teddy bears on the two beds. The whole place was spick and span and clean as a new pin. Considering the short time she must have had to prepare for a trip to Russia, she'd done well.

I poked around for a while until I found a spare front door key; then I moved a few things out of one of the drawers and unpacked. I stripped off and had myself a bath, liberally laced with some of the bath salts scattered all over the place. Then, wrapped in one of Anne's bath towels, I turned back one of the beds, lay down, and composed myself for a bit of heavy thinking.

Item one; how was I to get hold of Leo Tamir? He sure as hell wasn't going to answer any invitation, even if I knew where to deliver it. Item two; having sorted out item one, how was I going to manage the physical side of shipping him to Russia? Borensko had laid on all sorts of schemes for my approval, but a prime requisite for all of them was Leo himself. Item three; Having taken care of one and two, how was I going to make sure than Anne was returned safely? Item four; I fell asleep.

*   *   *

It was dark when I woke up and my watch had stopped. There wasn't much traffic outside, so it was fairly late. I wasn't interested enough to dial TIM and, finding an unopened bottle of vodka in the kitchen, I became even less interested. I started a list, heading it 'one bottle of vodka', which I left in the kitchen to be added to each time I swiped something else. Back in bed I started to marshal some of the random thought processes that had flitted back and forth on the edge of sleep. It was getting light outside and I'd killed half the bottle before I could honestly say that I had a rough idea of what I was going to do. 'Rough' was the operative word, and if ever there was a situation that was going to have to be played by ear, this was it. But at least I'd worked out stage one. Stage two could branch off in seventeen different directions, fifteen of which could turn out fatal for me. But fifteen to two were the best odds I could muster for the time being. I set the alarm for mid-day, pushed the bottle under the bed and started in on a little serious sleeping.

*   *   *

A bell jerked me awake. I was groping around for the alarm clock when I realised that it was the front door bell. This was a turn up for the book. I lay still, hoping whoever it was would go away eventually. But the bell continued to ring as though someone was leaning against it and had no intention of doing otherwise until the door was opened. So I clambered out of bed and, clutching the bath towel around me, I opened the front door. I'd quickly composed a story that I was Anne's uncle, down from the North for a week in the Smoke. But my story wasn't necessary. The two men outside the door had Max written all over them. As I opened the door, they stepped in without a word. The fact that they had to elbow me out of the way to do so, didn't worry them a bit. Not that I took much elbowing. With one hand clutching my modesty about me, I couldn't have resisted even if I'd wanted to. And, any-way, one didn't resist Max's Heavy Squad unless one wanted a broken arm at best, and a broken head at the other end of the scale. They were both large, hard-eyed men, neatly dressed and quietly spoken. I didn't know either of them. This wasn't surprising, because even in the old days when I'd worked for Max, I'd rarely had anything to do with the Heavy Squad.

Most of their work was conducted in sound proof rooms or anonymous alleyways.

One of them stood in the minute hall, keeping me company, while the other examined the apartment quickly. Then having ascertained that I was alone, I was prodded into the main room.

'Get dressed,' said Number One.

'Why?' I asked.

'Max wants to see you.'

'He'll have to wait,' I said.

'He wants to see you now.'

'So? He knows where I am.'

Number Two sighed gently, but Number One shook his head quickly. Obviously I wasn't to be thumped. Not yet anyway. 'He'd appreciate it if you could pay him a visit,' said Number One, obviously wishing he could belt me.

'I'll pop in and see him tomorrow,' I said.

Number One started to flounder a little. He'd been told to bring me in without bending me too much, and here I was being difficult. Number Two just looked nasty. 'He hoped you'd be able to see him right away.'

'Then he's going to be unlucky,' I said. 'Tell him I was coming to see him anyway. He owes me seven and a half thousand quid.'

The two men flashed a look at one another. This was news to them, as no doubt it would be to Max.

Number One made the final effort. 'We could fix an appointment for this afternoon,' he said hopefully.

'Ten-thirty tomorrow morning,' I said, heading for the front door. They shambled after me reluctantly. I opened the door and stood aside. 'Incidentally,' I said, as they moved past me. 'How did you know where I was?'

They looked at one another for a moment, then Number One shrugged as though it didn't matter. 'You were spotted out of Berlin,' he said.

I closed the door quietly behind them. I might just as well have caught a plane straight to London. But at least there was some satisfaction in knowing that Max must have tied up a dozen men to keep tabs on me from Paris, through to Le Touquet, across the Channel and into London. If nothing else I had given the tax payers a belting.

And having said I wouldn't go to see Max until next morning, I now had nothing to do. I'd intended calling on him that afternoon, but the fact that he had sent the Heavy Squad to fetch me had got up my nose. So let the bastard wait!

Now that he knew I was in circulation again, there didn't seem much point in staying at The Rabbit Warren. I dressed and packed, then I phoned the off-licence to send up a bottle of vodka to replace the one I had used. Because I was an evil bastard, with lecherous intent, I kept the spare key that I had found. I phoned the hire company and told them where they could pick up the car. Then I went home.

*   *   *

The flat smelled like a disused graveyard and looked just about as inviting. There was an even coating of dust over everything and a stale smell like a bad embalming job. A bottle of beer had iced up in the fridge and exploded. This had put the fridge out of commission so that a packet of frozen fish fingers had gone way off. It took me five minutes to locate the source of the smell and, when I finally opened the fridge door, I was practically knocked off my feet.

I slipped down to the local grocers, where along with bacon, eggs, bread and milk, I purchased one of those Fresh-Aire squirters. Back in the flat I sprayed it liberally over everything. It helped, but not much. Then I pulled out my battered old typewriter and started work. Many years before, I had decided that, as long as I was doing a dangerous job, I might as well take out some form of insurance. My insurance consisted of carefully documented reports about what I was doing, and what conclusions I drew. These reports I deposited in a safe deposit box in Switzerland. My long suffering London bank manager had the number of my deposit box and my instructions to open it should anything untoward happen to me. In the deposit box were detailed instructions as to what to do with the contents. If my head had rolled at any time, it would only have been the first of many, and Max's would have been close behind. It wasn't much as insurance policies go, but it had kept me alive through six years of working for Max, and six subsequent years, so it must have had something going for it.

I finished typing, sealed the stuff in an envelope, and addressed it to my Swiss bank. When I went out to buy stamps, there was a man sitting in a car twenty yards down from my front door. He could have been asleep, but I knew he wasn't. He followed me to the post office at a respectful distance, then back to my apartment. As I went in, he climbed back into his car to continue his vigil.

As my presence was now public knowledge, there seemed no point in keeping out of Mary's way any longer. I left it until eight, then showered and shaved and went to pay my respects. I'd like to have said that her expression when she opened the door to me was a compound of amazement and delight; but if it was, she concealed it admirably beneath a cloak of what can only be described as indifference.

'Hi!' she said. At least she stood aside to let me in. She allowed me to kiss her chastely, then she stood back and looked at me closely. 'You look terrible.'

'I've got the curse,' I said, trying to make light of something that was annoying me no end.

'You've been having yourself quite a time,' she said. 'You made page one.'

'I'm surprised you noticed,' I said, miffed as hell.

'Fifteen years wasn't it?'

'Time flies,' I sparkled.

'Indeed it does. I expected you yesterday.'

I really was surprised at this, and said so.

'Two unpleasant gentlemen called on me and said if you contacted me, I was to let them know,' she said. That was Max again. Not content with tailing me clear across Europe, he had been making sure that if I slipped his tail, there'd be no place for me to go. Which only goes to show how little he knew Mary.

'Do you want to know what happened?' I asked.

'No,' she said firmly. Then she softened sufficiently to qualify the remark. 'What I don't know can't hurt me. And I don't want to get hurt any more because of you.'

I wasn't aware that I'd managed to hurt her already, and I said so.

'Because you're a fat, balding, insensitive bastard,' she said. Fat and balding I may have been, but I was sensitive enough to know that I wasn't insensitive.

She turned on me about then. 'You pop in and out of my life like a bloody yo-yo. And I'm supposed to be happy and grateful to see you every time you condescend to put in an appearance.' I started to say something, but she stopped me, in full flow now. 'And it's no good saying you don't make demands on me. Just being there is the biggest demand of the lot. You put on your whipped spaniel look and I start thinking I'm a first water bitch. Well I'm not, and I don't like being made to feel guilty for something that isn't any of my doing.'

The evening wasn't going at all the way I had planned, and I began to panic a little. 'I love you, you know that,' I said, casting caution to the wind.

'No, you don't,' she said. 'If you did, you'd ask me to marry you.'

'So marry me,' I said, completely demented by now.

'I wouldn't marry you if you were the last man on earth,' she said. In a lifetime of dealing with illogicals, I'd never learned to fathom the illogicality of women, because suddenly she smiled and it was like the sun coming out.

'But at least you asked me,' she said.

I admitted that I'd asked her, failing to get the point.

'You're a bastard most of the time,' she said. 'But you're rather sweet.' She patted my cheek affectionately, rather like she would have done one of her horses.

'Dinner or bed?' she said.

'Bed,' I said, getting back to firmer ground.

'No,' she countered. 'Dinner.' And she started to strip off. I made a tentative grab at her as she padded across to the bathroom, but she evaded me easily. 'After dinner will be better,' she said. 'Booze improves your performance.'

'I can booze now,' I said, beginning to work up a forni-

148

cator's sweat. But she disappeared into the bathroom, and in case I hadn't got the message, she locked the door loudly behind her.

*　　*　　*

So we dined leisurely in one of our regular restaurants, while the manager frantically searched for a bill I had run up that he hadn't expected to collect on for fifteen years. When he presented it to me, all he said was that it was nice to see me back. It was that sort of restaurant, all candelabra and discretion. We played footsy under the table while Mary tucked away a meal that would have done justice to an Irish navvy, and during the sweet and the coffee I began to champ at the bit. I paid the bill and galloped Mary back to her apartment and into bed. It was like coming home again. Familiarity may breed contempt in some areas, but as far as I was concerned, the familiarity of Mary's warm, gentle, body bred only affection and extreme gratitude. Afterwards I lay smoking while she idly picked fluff out of my navel.

'Was it terrible?' she said.

'It was sensational.'

'Not me, idiot! Russia.'

'It wasn't too bad,' I said.

'Why did they let you go?'

This I couldn't tell her. No doubt there'd be something about it in the newspapers tomorrow, put there by Max. But until I knew what story he was going to concoct, I could do nothing but keep quiet.

Mary didn't seem to mind when I didn't tell her and, after an hour, she pushed me out of bed.

'Why can't I stay?' I asked.

149

'Because the bed's too small, and you snore. To-night I've got to sleep, I've got a heavy day tomorrow.'

She was right about the bed being too small. I'd been on at her for longer than I could remember to get a double bed. But she said that, as a single girl, a double bed would give the impression that she was promiscuous. I think the true reason she didn't have a double bed was her fear that I might move in with her permanently, but we kept up the pretence. The odd nights I *had* stayed had invariably been sleepless ones for both of us.

I got dressed reluctantly and kissed her good-bye. She was asleep before I was out of the flat. I was using my own car now and, before going home, I drove to Fleet Street and picked up a copy of tomorrow's paper. Max had excelled himself. There was a terrible picture of me on page one with a story that said that due to the vast improvement in East-West relationships the Russians, not wanting to throw a spanner in the works, had decided to be magnanimous and suspend my sentence, provided I never returned to any of the Iron Curtain countries. That would hand Borensko a laugh. But as far as he was concerned, they could say what they bloody well liked; none of the people who mattered would believe a word of it anyway. My watcher, or his double, was still parked outside my apartment, and I saw him acknowledge receipt of me to the man who had followed me for the entire evening. Max was taking no chances of my failing to keep my appointment.

*   *   *

I turned up promptly at ten-thirty and was shown straight into Max's office. He was sniffing away at an inhaler when I came in. He smiled apologetically at me as he put it away and mopped his streaming eyes. 'Doctor said it might be better than eye drops,' he said.

I hoped fervently that the doctor didn't know what he was talking about; one of the few pleasures left in life was watching Max suffer. While he was mopping up the deluge, he pushed a newspaper across the desk towards me.

'I've seen it,' I said.

'Good?'

'Adequate.'

'So what happened?'

'They let me go,' I said.

'Why?'

'With Antonov dead, there was no point in keeping me.'

'They didn't arrest you because of Antonov.'

'But that was the whole idea, wasn't it?'

'You and I know it,' said Max. 'They didn't.'

'They do now,' I said. 'I told them.'

Max leaned back in his chair, his hands flat on the desk in front of him. The clock on the wall ticked away a noisy minute.

'Mmm,' said Max.

'I'm sorry,' I said. 'But I didn't feel up to doing fifteen years.'

'You told them that the whole job was a frame?'

'I did.'

'And they let you go?'

'They did.'

'You're a liar.'

'So I'm a liar, and please can I have the rest of my money?'

Max grinned, a thoroughly unpleasant baring of his immaculate teeth. 'You're joking of course.'

'What do you think?'

'You're not joking?'

'Right,' I said. 'Cash please, no cheques.'

'Did they knock you about?'

'Some,' I admitted.

Max nodded thoughtfully. 'I thought so,' he said. 'You've had a bash on the head, it's affected your thought processes.'

'You'll have to do better than that.'

'So try this,' said Max. 'I slap a lien on your bank account and get back the twenty-five per cent I've already paid you.'

'But you won't do that.'

'Why won't I.' He was still smiling.

'Seller's market,' I said.

He put his teeth away. 'What's the commodity?' he asked.

I shook my head. 'It's not for you.'

'For who?'

'Your friends in the CIA.'

Now he started to look nasty. 'What have you got that they might buy?' he asked.

'Not might,' I said. 'Will.'

'What?'

'I'll tell the customer. In the meantime, give me my seven and half thousand quid and I promise not to spill too much mud over your name.'

'It's been muddied before,' he said.

'Not with the brand of mud I'll use.'

'You're bluffing, John,' he said.

I got to my feet. 'Suit yourself,' I said. 'But I'll get it in the end. If not from you, from the CIA.'

I started for the door, then I remembered something. I turned back. 'Incidentally, what did Antonov die from?'

'A coronary,' said Max. I thought I saw a momentary flash

152

of something in his eyes, but it could have been the water that was still streaming out. 'Don't try to treat the CIA like you treat me,' he added, just before I went through the door. 'They're hard cases when they need to be.'

'You're frightening me to death,' I said. And I left.

I hadn't for a moment expected to get any money from Max but at least I'd got him wondering, which was the purpose of my visit. I'd also rattled him a little by way of a bonus. Now all I had to do was to wait for the CIA to contact me. I knew that they would. Max would see to that, even if it was only to satisfy his own curiosity as to what I was up to.

*   *   *

They didn't take long either. I'd been home for an hour when there was a polite tap on the door and I opened it to two of my American cousins. CIA men come in all shapes and sizes. There are the part timers, who do other, normal-type work; then there are the scholarly individuals who work with computers and such like in the offices that the CIA run all over the world; there are CIA men disguised as soldiers, Peace Corps workers, students, minor diplomats, and plain common or garden tourists. But somewhere behind this bunch there is the hard core of professionals, who do the dirty and the dangerous work. And, with my luck, it was a natural that I should draw two of these.

As they removed their topcoats they introduced themselves. Harvey Dacron was six feet two inches, slim and sporting a crew cut; Martin Rich was shorter by a good few inches, more heavily built, and nearly bald. Both wore neat, navy blue, light-weight suits, and button down shirts with plain knitted ties. They could have been anything from Madison

Avenue to Wall Street. They were polite, almost deferential, and they would have cut my throat as soon as look at me. Martin Rich had obviously been elected spokesman and, while he chatted me up, Harvey meandered around the apartment, apparently aimlessly, but in fact making sure I didn't have the place wired for sound. There's something almost pathological in the way Americans expect everything to be bugged; to me, a bug is something you find in a dirty bed and I didn't know one end of a tape recorder from the other. But while Martin talked inconsequentials, Harvey ran an unobtrusive, but thorough, check over my establishment. Obviously satisfied, he gave Martin an invisible sign, and business started.

'Max said you wanted to see us, John,' said Martin with the customary American irreverence for anything but christian names.

'I didn't say that.'

'He said you'd got something to sell us,' prodded Martin.

'I hadn't anticipated making contact as soon as this,' I lied. There was no point in letting them take over the entire proceedings. But I hadn't allowed for that old American 'get up and go'.

Martin persisted gently. 'There's no time like the present. That's what we always say, eh Harvey?' Harvey nodded. He wasn't really listening; he was watching me through a pair of the clearest blue eyes I'd ever seen. He looked as though he were measuring me for a box. 'So suppose you tell us what it is you're selling, and we'll tell you if we're interested in buying.'

'You'll buy all right,' I said. 'But I can't sell to you personally.'

There was a moment's pause.

'To whom then?' said Martin finally.

'Leo Tamir,' I said, holding my breath. I needn't have bothered. They accepted it without batting an eyelid.

'When do you want to see him?'

About here I should have started to get suspicious, but I was so relieved at having crossed what I had anticipated as a nasty hurdle that my natural mistrust of Americans in general and the CIA in particular took a back seat.

'Just have him call me,' I said. 'I'll arrange the meeting with him direct.'

'Why not give us the details?' said Martin. 'It'll save time.'

'Time I've plenty of,' I said. 'Just have him call me.'

There was another pause while Martin digested this. Then Harvey decided to take an interest in the proceedings.

'What's so special about Tamir?' he asked.

'Nothing special about him,' I said. 'Just that what I've got to sell I'm only going to sell to him.'

'He won't have the money with him,' said Martin.

'Don't you trust him yet?' I enquired lightly.

Martin smiled gently. 'You know better than that, John. Like you, we don't trust anybody.' It was the first really sensible thing he'd said since he arrived.

'If Tamir isn't allowed to carry money, how do I get paid?' I asked, not unreasonably I thought.

'You give him sufficient information for head office to judge whether it's worth the price you're asking. If it is, another meeting will be arranged. You can give him the balance of the information and he'll give you the money.'

'So you *do* trust him to carry money,' I said.

'Of course we do,' said Martin.

'It's you we have doubts about,' said Harvey. 'If Tamir is carrying twenty-five thousand dollars with him first time round, what's to stop you banging him on the head and making off with it?'

There were all sorts of loose ends to this argument, but I let them all go while I seized on the point that really interested me.

'Who said anything about twenty-five thousand dollars,' I asked.

'It was just a figure of speech,' said Martin.

'Then try figuring your speech up near the hundred thousand mark.'

Martin looked sad. 'That's a lot of money John,' he said.

'I've a lot to sell.'

'Perhaps. Perhaps not. We shall see. After we know what it is, then will be the time for haggling about the price.'

'Sounds fair,' I lied. 'I'll wait to hear from him then.'

I started towards the door to show them out. Harvey was standing in my way and he didn't move. 'You wouldn't be putting us on, would you, John?' he said.

'Why on earth should I do that, Harvey?' I asked, with righteous indignation.

'I don't know,' said Harvey. 'But I don't like the smell.'

'Some fish fingers went off,' I said, realising that he wasn't quite as simple as the button down shirt and crew cut implied.

Martin came up behind me. 'Harvey is merely intimating that should all not be as it seems, there could be trouble. Serious trouble.'

'Trouble's my middle name,' I said.

'Not our sort of trouble, John, believe you me,' said Martin politely, and the two of them let themselves out of the door as quietly as they had entered. 'Bay of Pigs to you,' I muttered as I closed the door behind them.

*   *   *

156

That seemed to be that. Wheels had been set in motion and all I could do now was to wait. But while waiting I decided to investigate the gleam I had spotted in Max's eye when I had mentioned the death of Antonov. It fitted in with an idea I had formulated somewhere along the line, but which I had rejected as being too far out, even for Max. On consideration I remembered that there was nothing too far out for Max. So I went and bought some back-copy newspapers. Being a bit of a masochist, I bought editions that covered my arrest and trial, as well as those I needed. The whole trial bit was a fascinating exercise in journalistic double talk. It was obviously a big story at the time, but D notices had been issued to cover various portions of it, and so the facts were liberally laced with fiction. There were a couple of indignant editorials and a number of interviews with political pundits and foreign correspondents, whose opinions of the fiasco ranged from indignant disapproval of the British for employing such a stupid person as John Smith right through to outrage that the Russians should arrest an innocent British tractor salesman, even if he were a spy. The colour of the reporting was governed solely by the political shade of the particular newspaper, and none of them from *The Times* to the *Morning Star* had the remotest idea what they were talking about.

But reading all this provided a pleasant enough interlude prior to getting down to work. The work in question involved learning as much as I could about the death of Antonov. As a man recently arrested for spying, his obituaries were decidedly sparse. Briefly it boiled down to the fact that while he was in prison awaiting trial on umpteen counts under the Official Secrets Act, he had suffered a heart attack. He'd been transferred to the prison hospital, where he had lingered for a couple of days before giving up the ghost. It all sounded very simple and straightforward. But there was a nasty smell somewhere and it had nothing to do with fish fingers.

I searched out one particular report and then made a phone call. The call was to the author of the report, who had gently hinted that perhaps all was not as it should be. He'd obviously had his knuckles rapped later, because there was no follow up. Half an hour later I answered the door to Fred Terry, a sometime freelance newspaper man, and a not-very-often novelist. We'd known each other on and off for a long time. I'd saved his life once by marrying the girl he was going steady with. He must have recognised her for what she was long before I came on the scene because, instead of taking umbrage when I appeared with flowers and chocolates, he treated me like the best friend he'd ever had. We'd met on and off during the disastrous five years of my marriage and during the divorce we'd almost become bosom buddies. We'd spend hours talking about the failings of women in general, and our common link in particular. After that we went our separate ways again, meeting only now and then. I'd steered him into a couple of stories before anyone else knew of their development and he had pointed me in the direction of some minor jobs which helped pay the rent. Also, he had introduced me to Mary and, even if I'd hated his guts, I had to be grateful for that.

He's a long, gangling man, with arms and legs sticking out every whichway. He holds his head slightly to one side as though he is listening for something all the time. All in all he looks like a human assembly kit that has been badly put together, which one good shove would cause to fall apart. But behind his ragbag appearance there was a reasoning mind of sorts and, in my telephoning him, he sensed a story. So thirty minutes after I hung up on him, he was spread all around one of my armchairs clutching a drink.

'The traveller returns,' he said. 'What happened?'

'Don't you read your newspapers?'

'They only print the sort of balls I write. Are you going to give me a story?'

'You couldn't use it even if I did. They'd lock you up.'

'Not even a little story?'

'Perhaps, but later,' I said. 'Right now I want a favour.'

He downed his drink rapidly and started to wind himself up preparatory to getting to his feet. 'Favours for you usually involve someone getting their head bent,' he said. 'I'll see you around.'

But I bullied him into hearing me out and, after he'd probed around for a while trying to dig the grain of an idea from what I was asking, he agreed to help me. There wasn't any need for him to make such a big deal about it as all I was asking for was a couple of introductions. He knew it, too, but he made drama out of it so that the next time he asked me for a favour the ledger would be well balanced in his column. I went along with him, slapping him on the back a couple of times and telling him what a good fellow he was. He made some phone calls and a meeting was set up. Just before he left he remembered something. 'There's a fellow outside watching this place,' he said.

'Nothing to do with me,' I told him. 'They're running a brothel in the flat upstairs and the law can't decide whether to do anything about it.'

'He didn't look like a policeman,' said Fred, suspiciously.

'Vice squad never do,' I said, pushing him out of the door. I watched him gangle down the stairs, no wiser and a little drunker than he had been when he arrived.

*   *   *

The meeting Fred had arranged was for that evening, and this was one get-together that I didn't want Max to know about. So, two hours before the appointed time, I put on my coat and went out to lose my tail.

Unfortunately I chose to go out just as the shifts were changing over, and the off-going worker decided to put in a bit of overtime helping his mate. This gave me two to contend with, which is infinitely more difficult than one. Anyone can lose one tail, but with two men on the job, one can follow you into the shop, while the other goes round and covers the back door; one can travel on the same bus with you, while the other follows in a taxi; one can make a call for reinforcements while the other keeps tabs. It's a difficult operation which requires a little thought and concentration; particularly in this case as they didn't mind one little bit that I knew they were tailing me. This allowed them practically to sit in my pocket. So I played it cool for the first half hour, lulling them into a sense of false security. This put me in Oxford Street at rush hour, where a man with three heads could lose himself in the crowd if he had a mind to.

I joined the commuters battling their way into Oxford Circus tube station where I bought a ticket while Mutt and Jeff queued three places behind me, buying theirs. I managed to insinuate a few more people between me and them on the down escalator. Just before we reached the bottom, a train came in and a great mob of people poured towards the up escalator. I made it just ahead of them and, by the time Mutt and Jeff crossed over, there were thirty to forty people jammed between us. My way ahead was clear and I started to mount the moving staircase two at a time. I heard once that this is bad for the heart. It didn't do my heart any harm, but it must have played havoc with Mutt and Jeff's.

At the top of the escalator, I crossed back to the downside. We were only ten feet away from each other when we passed, going in opposite directions. But they were so busy looking upwards to where I had disappeared and trying to shove their way through the crowd that they didn't even see me.

At the bottom, I caught a train and got out one station later at Regents Park. There I picked up a cab and gave him the address that Fred had given me.

It was an insalubrious looking pub and Fred was waiting for me in the saloon bar. With him was a sad little man with a large moustache and boils on the back of his neck. Fred introduced us, then discreetly withdrew to chew his fingernails, while I got down to business.

*   *   *

Two hours later I was back home. Jeff had gone, no doubt regretting his offer to put in some overtime, but Mutt was still there and he glared at me as I got out of my cab. He'd be getting a rocket up his ass from Max tomorrow and, if he could have jumped on my face right there, he would have done so happily. But what Max was going to do to him was nothing to what I was going to do to Max. My little man with the boils had turned over a large stone for me and what I had found underneath was just about as nasty as anything I'd come across for a long time.

CHAPTER SEVEN

TAMIR CALLED me the following day.

'Mr Smith, this is Leo Tamir,' he said when I answered the phone.

'Hello, Leo, how's the stomach?'

'Not good, Mr Smith. You want to see me I understand?'

'That's the general idea,' I said. 'When can you make it?'

'I am at your service.'

I arranged to meet him at the White City Greyhound Racing Stadium. Being a Saturday, the place would be crowded enough to be anonymous and noisy enough to prevent anyone from overhearing our conversation. I telephoned the restaurant to reserve a table; as long as we were going to talk we might as well eat while we were doing it.

I then wrote a cheque for one thousand pounds and trotted round to my bank to cash it. The teller looked at me a little cross-eyed when I pushed it across the counter at him but, after a hurried consultation with the manager, he paid me out with one hundred ten pound notes. I left the bank feeling much better. If Max was going to block my bank account, he wasn't going to find much economical advantage.

Having nothing further to do until the evening, I went to my office. Harvey Stubbs was a five day week man, so Miss Roberts wasn't there either. I let myself in and, after hanging up my coat, I searched through Miss Roberts' desk until I found the file where she had stored my mail. I carried it through to my own office, put my feet on the desk and proceeded to catch up on the last few weeks.

There were a few bills, for which I promptly wrote cheques; there was a note from Phil Bannister thanking me for pushing some business his way; and there was a small cheque from a client I thought had died. That and a dozen pamphlets was the sum total of my absence. I left a note for Miss Roberts saying I wouldn't be in for a couple of weeks as I needed a holiday after my shattering experience. Then I shut up shop and went to see Solly Weisman.

Solly runs a clock and watch repair shop, just off Cheapside. At least, clocks and watches are the front; in the back you can buy anything from a Bren gun down to a bow and arrow. He could probably have provided a Polaris missile if your references were good and you had the money to pay for it. He was the armourer for the local villains, reliable, tightlipped and very expensive. But only expensive to everyone else; I got what I wanted for free. Somewhere back in the dim distant past, I had stumbled on the fact that Solly had deserted from the British army during the war. I used this piece of information whenever I needed hardware to bolster up my courage. This wasn't often because, while I didn't have much courage most of the time, my antipathy towards guns usually outweighed my cowardice. I don't like guns and I never have; as a functional piece of equipment I suppose they have their uses, but my recipe for a long and healthy life is to stay out of situations where guns are needed. Still, there came times when even I felt the need of outside support and this was one of those times.

While Solly watched me through his sad Jewish eyes, I took

my pick of what was in the back room. I chose a Smith and Wesson .38 police special and twenty-five rounds of ammunition. I drew the ammunition from a box holding two hundred rounds. I didn't want Solly picking out the cartridges for me; he'd as soon have put talcum powder in them as gunpowder. I was the only link with his past, the only person who knew about his desertion, and it offended his Jewish peace of mind. It bothered him not one little bit that what he was doing every day could put him inside for ten years. As far as he was concerned, what he was now engaged in was honest villainy, whereas desertion had a sneaky connotation quite out of proportion to the gravity of the charge. Also there was the knowledge that his customers were villains themselves and would cheerfully have cut their own throats before grassing. Whereas I wasn't a villain. A bastard maybe, but I would have sung like Nelly Melba if it would have got me out of trouble. And Solly knew it.

So he watched me sadly as I took my pick of his stock, and tried to talk me into taking a holster as well. A holster is for the birds, or for people who carry guns without expecting ever to have to use them. They are nasty dangerous things which are liable to snag in the gun at the critical moment leaving blood over everything. And, while I hoped fervently that I wasn't going to have to use the gun, at least if I did have to, I had no intention of cluttering myself up with a holster. So I declined Solly's offer politely, tucked my acquisition deep in my raincoat pocket, and left Solly wishing he could shoot me in the back.

*   *   *

Tamir was right on time. We met outside the restaurant entrance to the White City, where I bought two tickets. We went straight upstairs and were shown to the table I had reserved. The first race was about to start and, while Leo looked around the place and wondered what on earth he'd choose from the menu that wouldn't upset his stomach, I trotted up to the tote window and laid out a little of my hard-earned money. By the time I got back to my table the race was over and I'd struck lucky. This meant I had to go back and collect my winnings. While I was doing this, I bumped into someone I knew vaguely and we talked for five minutes, so by the time I got back to the table once more, it was time to bet for the next race. All in all, three quarters of an hour passed before Leo could pin me down to any sort of talking.

He did so finally, while I was noshing into an *escalope Holstein*, and he was toying with some boiled fish.

'Please, Mr Smith. I am not enjoying myself and I would like to get down to business.'

'I'm having a ball,' I said. 'I've won a hundred pounds already.'

'I'm glad,' he said. 'Perhaps now you will tell me what it is you wish to see me about.'

'Don't you know?'

'Only that you have something to sell and that you will deal only with me. What I can't understand is . . .'

I cut in on him quickly. 'I didn't say I would deal only with you. I said I would sell only to you.'

'But why?'

'Because you're the person with the most interest in buying.'

His flat eyes became even flatter. He toyed a moment with his revolting looking meal, then pushed it aside. 'What you are trying to say is that the CIA would not be interested, but that I, as an individual, would.'

'I didn't say they wouldn't be interested. It's just that you would be more interested.'

'Please get to the point, Mr Smith.'

'I spent some time with Borensko,' I said.

There was a moment's pause. 'So?' he said finally.

'He told me all about you,' I said.

'What did he tell you?'

I flashed a look over my shoulder then leaned forward conspiratorially. 'You don't have to worry,' I said. 'I'm on your side.'

He'd not the slightest idea what I was talking about and he said so.

'Come on, Leo,' I said. 'I know you're working for Borensko.'

If I'd emptied my *Holstein* over his lap he couldn't have looked more surprised. I reached across and patted his arm. 'You certainly had me fooled,' I said.

He pulled his arm away from my hand. 'You are talking nonsense,' he said. 'Dangerous nonsense.'

'It's not dangerous as long as only you and I know about it.'

'This was what you wanted to see me about?'

I sat back. 'What else?' I said.

He looked at me steadily for a while and it was only by conjuring up a vision of the umpteen people he had murdered that I was able to stop myself from feeling sorry for him.

'I believe you know this isn't true,' he said finally. 'The problem that now confronts me is – why?'

'Yes,' I agreed. 'It's quite a problem.'

'I am realistic enough to know that if you told my present employers, it would cause me a great deal of trouble.'

'Indeed it would.'

'Regardless of whether or not it is true.'

'Regardless,' I agreed.

'So the problem resolves itself purely on the basis of how much money you will accept.'

'No,' I said.

Then I left him for a few minutes to make another bet. When I returned he hadn't moved and he picked up the conversation as though it hadn't been interrupted.

'Why not?' he asked.

'It goes deeper than that,' I said. 'I may be working for Borensko myself, but there is the faintest chance that he is lying to me and you are telling the truth.'

I thought I saw a flash of hope in his eyes, but it was extinguished immediately.

'So?' he said.

'So I'm going to give you a chance to get out.'

'Why?'

'Because you're going to pay me,' I said.

'And if I don't?'

'Then no doubt the CIA will hear about your defection. And as you say, true or not, it can only bring you trouble.'

'What's your price?'

'A hundred thousand dollars. Fifty for you and fifty for me.'

He almost smiled. 'And where am I going to get a hundred thousand dollars?' he asked.

'You're here to negotiate with me on behalf of the CIA so negotiate.'

'You'll have to have something worth selling first.'

'I can give you the names of three officers on the NATO staff, none below the rank of colonel, who all work for Borensko. I can give you the sailing orders of two of their nuclear submarines, both working off the Newfoundland coast. And, best of all, I can give them *you*, unless you can convince them that what I am selling is worth the money.'

A waiter grabbed his boiled fish and pushed an ice cream under his nose. He wasn't even aware of it. He was looking at me steadily, hate oozing from his eyes.

'Why are you doing all this?' he asked finally.

'I like money. I don't like you. And I don't like Borensko, even if I do work for him.'

He glanced down at the ice cream, then pushed it aside and stood up.

'You'll hear from me,' he said.

I smiled at him. 'I'm sure I will.'

I watched him as he threaded his way through the tables towards the elevators. There was one simple solution to his problem and I didn't believe for a moment that he hadn't thought about it. Killing used to come easy to him and there was no reason why an upset stomach should have spoiled his aim. Until I next heard from him I was going to have to be very careful. Apart from murdering me, there was no way out for him other than what I had suggested. He knew he wasn't working for Borensko, and he'd a pretty good idea that I knew it too. But a word to the CIA would be all that was needed to have him put away permanently. Even if they weren't fully convinced, they couldn't afford to take that sort of chance. After all, he'd done an about-face once before. There would be a quiet little accident somewhere, which might make a page two story in a local paper, and that would be that. In effect, I was blackmailing him with material that didn't exist. It was a pretty fanciful idea and it couldn't have happened to a better person than Leo Tamir.

I stayed for the next couple of races, paid for dinner, and left. I had a medium sized alcoholic glow on me, I'd won fifty quid, and the necessary wheels had already been spun into motion. Life was good, and getting better. Wait until Anne Ballard learned what I was going through on her behalf; she'd be so bloody grateful it would be sickening.

*   *   *

In fact I was feeling so good, I didn't even mind when Leo tried to kill me. He'd obviously allowed American culture to get the better of his original training, because what he tried was straight out of prohibition. I had picked up my car from the car park and was driving slowly back into town when this car ran into the back of me at the traffic lights. It wasn't a large bash, but sufficient for me to switch off the engine and get out to go and inspect the damage. My fender was badly bent as was the panelling at the rear. Preparing to swap insurance companies I walked towards the car that had done the damage. I realised that there was no driver behind the wheel – and at the same time I saw Leo. He had obviously climbed out of the car on the passenger side and was now leaning in through the passenger window for all the world like an interested bystander looking to see what it was all about. I was supposed to lean in through the window on the driver's side and get a face full of bullet. Instead I moved round behind him and, before he knew what was happening, I had grasped his arms just below the elbows, keeping his hands shoved deep in his topcoat pockets. His arms were like matchsticks, which goes to show what a diet of boiled fish can do for a man. I made a disapproving, clucking sound.

'Silly man, Leo,' I said. 'You must know me better than that.'

Suddenly the stiffness went out of him. People were gathering now, and I could see a bucket shaped helmet bobbing towards us over the heads of the crowd. I released Leo's arms and he turned towards me, pulling his empty hands from his pockets. He looked almost embarrassed.

'You're right, Mr Smith,' he said. 'It was stupid. But only because it didn't work.'

'Never mind,' I said, consolingly. The policeman was nearly with us by now. 'But in case you feel like trying it again, I've got it all written down.'

I don't know whether he believed me or not because the policeman finally got through to us. 'Have to move those cars, gentlemen, he said. 'Blocking the traffic.'

'Certainly, officer,' I said in my best public spirited voice.

'And you, sir,' he said to Leo. Leo looked at him blankly.

'It's not my car, officer,' he said. Obviously he'd knocked it off in the White City car park, just to follow me. While the policeman was looking round for the non-existent driver, Leo gave me a small nod and started to push his way out through the crowd.

The policeman took my name and address and radioed his mates that he'd found an abandoned car. The patrol car arrived and more details were taken. Finally, an hour later, I was allowed to go about my business.

*   *   *

I drove home, parked the car, and let myself into my apartment. Max was sitting in my best armchair. There were two of his Heavy Squad with him. One was going through the bureau where I kept my unpaid bills and the other appeared in the doorway of my bedroom as I let myself in. All three of

170

them were looking at me steadily and I decided to play it very cool indeed.

'Come on in, John,' said Max generously. 'Sit down.'

I took off my coat and sat.

'What are you up to, John?' he said when he thought I was comfortable.

'I told you yesterday,' I said.

He waved my answer away with his hand. 'What are you really up to?'

'Making a living,' I said.

'By selling information to the CIA?' I nodded. 'Not good enough, John. Not good enough at all.'

'Then you tell me,' I said.

He leaned forward. 'Let's try this,' he said. 'You're working for Borensko.'

'Who's Borensko?'

He treated this with the contempt which it deserved, ignoring it completely. 'You made some sort of deal with him to let you go. I want to know what that deal is.'

'If you find out, be sure to tell me,' I said.

He sighed gently and pulled out his eyedrops. I was glad to see the inhaler hadn't done him any good. I waited while he squirted more liquid into his already streaming eyes. And while I was waiting I hoped that his two associates wouldn't decide to poke around in my raincoat pocket. The gun was still there. But hopes like that usually turn out to be futile. Before Max had even put away his handkerchief, one of his men brought him my gun and the ammunition. He looked at it as the man held it out to him, butt first. But he didn't touch it. He looked at me again.

'A gun, John?'

I admitted it was a gun.

'Not like you. Not like you at all,' he said, like he was disappointed. 'What's it for?'

'To shoot people,' I said. He smiled, a thin exposure of his teeth.

'Like who?'

'Like you, if you don't take your two boys and get your ass out of here.'

He shook his head slowly. 'It wouldn't be for Leo Tamir would it?' he said.

'I've already shot him once.'

'To stop him from shooting you?'

'Now why would he want to do that?' I said, beginning to feel uncomfortable.

'I can think of a number of reasons,' said Max.

'You could think of reasons for a man to shoot his own mother,' I said, trying to head him away from the course the conversation was taking.

'Does Borensko want Leo killed?' asked Max. 'Is that the bargain you made with him?'

'Who's Borensko?' I said, flogging a dead horse.

He sat forward, putting his hands on his knees. An edge came into his voice, a cutting edge. 'Leo Tamir works for the CIA,' he said. 'While he is over here, he comes under my protection. I'm responsible for him. If anything happens to him it would cause me considerable inconvenience.'

This was a bonus as far as I was concerned. To cause Max inconvenience was as good as a holiday. But I decided that the conversation had gone far enough. I didn't think Max had anything to go on, he was just fishing. So I decided to call his bluff and get ugly. 'I don't give a fuck for Leo Tamir,' I said.

'And I don't give a fuck for you or your two boys here. If you want to pinch me for having a gun, go ahead. But I don't have to sit here and listen to any more balls from you and I don't intend to. So if you've got anything bright and scintillating to say, say it quick before I throw you all out.'

I could feel a tightening of the atmosphere in the room, a backwash caused by the heavy boys flexing their muscles. I braced myself for a thump from behind, all the time watching Max in case I could recognise a signal which would give me time to take evasive action. But no signal came. Max sat where he was for a moment longer; then he got to his feet slowly and headed for the door. His men beat him to it and opened it for him. Just before he went out he turned back to me. 'Be careful, John,' he said. And he was gone.

I poured myself a drink, and it wasn't until I'd downed it that I saw they had left my gun on the table. I felt unreasonably pleased with myself. Max had dropped a clanger. His visit went towards confirming something I was already three parts sure of, and made what was to follow a whole lot easier.

*   *   *

I spent the next couple of days just hanging around waiting for Leo to contact me. My apartment was still being watched so, to relieve the boredom, I played games with the men whose job it was to shadow me everywhere, losing them time and time again. After the third time I was gratified to see that they had doubled the watch. This made the game even more interesting, and I spent a fortune on bus and taxi fares, getting a childish satisfaction each time I managed to slip out from under.

On the third day I was letting myself into the flat after leaving two men stranded on top of the Post Office tower, when the phone started to ring. I answered it.

'This is Leo Tamir.'

'Hello, Leo,' I said affably.

'My employers like the sound of your commodity and they agree to your price.'

'Good,' I said. Then because I knew that he was waiting for me to continue, I let him sweat a little and said nothing. The silence grew as I listened to his breathing on the other end of the phone.

'Are you still there, Mr Smith?' he said finally.

'I'm still here, Leo,' I said.

'The arrangements, please?' he said. This required a bit of thought. It was better than fifty-fifty that my line was being tapped and Leo would know this. Therefore, the arrangements he wanted to hear were those designed for public consumption; namely an official exchange of money for information, all normal and above board. The arrangements I was supposed to have made for him personally, whereby he could abscond with fifty thousand dollars of the CIA's money, were for his ears alone; he would expect me to tell him about these later.

'You come here,' I said. 'The key's under the mat. Be here at six-thirty exactly.' Before he could say anything else, I hung up.

*   *   *

At five o'clock I went out. My two tails were waiting for me and they dutifully followed me to the nearest call box. There I made a call to a number that Borensko had given me. I came out of the call box, nodded politely to the two men, who were propping up the railings, and went into the pub.

There I sat, supping ale until exactly six-thirty. The two

shadows were at the other side of the bar, trying to stretch one drink as far as they could and trying to look everywhere except at me. At six-thirty I borrowed sixpence from the barman and went to use the pub phone. I dialled my own number. It rang ten times before Leo answered it. He was out of breath, apparently having run upstairs. I didn't give him a chance to say anything once he had identified himself.

'O.K.?' I said.

'Yes, Mr Smith. O.K.,' he replied, and hung up. I'd left a note under the mat with the key, telling him where to meet me. Now it was up to him. If there was a tail on him he'd have to lose it. That was his problem. Mine was in the shape of the two men who had followed me into the pub. Clutching my own drink, I went to join them at the bar. At first they tried to pretend I wasn't there; but eventually they realised they were looking rather stupid, so they accepted my invitation.

'Thank you, sir, I'll have a bitter,' said the larger of the two.

The smaller looked a little panicky for a moment, then he also nodded. 'Same for me, please.'

I bought and paid for their drinks, wished them good health and then got down to business.

'Which one of you is in charge?' I asked.

They looked at one another, then the large one turned to me. 'I am,' he said.

'What's your name?'

'I don't think that's . . .'

'It doesn't really matter,' I said, cutting in. 'I'll call you Fred.'

'It's Jim,' he said. I looked at the little one.

'Bob,' he said, as though he were ashamed of it.

'All right, Jim,' I said. 'Here's what I want you to do. You go and phone Max while Bob here keeps his eye on me. You tell Max that unless I walk out of here in five minutes, leaving you two propping up the bar, I'm going to get on to our mutual friend on the other side and tell him what I know about Antonov.'

Jim looked at me empty-eyed for a moment. I could see the wheels beginning to turn in his head. 'I'm sorry, sir, I don't know what you're talking about,' he managed finally.

'Have you ever seen Max when he's got the needle?' I asked. It was obvious that he had. 'So be a good lad and do what I say. I'm walking out of here in five minutes – *alone*, O.K.?'

He looked at Bob for help, but got none. Then, weighing up the pros and cons, he made up his mind. He borrowed six-pence from Bob and lumbered off to telephone. Left alone with me, Bob was even more embarrassed than he had been at first.

'How did you like the view from the Post Office Tower?' I asked. He'd have liked to have glowered at me, but he was unsure of his ground, so he contented himself with grunting an unintelligible monosyllable into his beer.

Three minutes later Jim returned, looking red in the face. He ignored me completely. 'Come on Bob,' he said. 'We're off duty.' Bob started to down the remainder of his drink.

'Me first,' I said. 'And give me ten minutes.'

He nodded unhappily and I left them at the bar, two cogs in a wheel which obviously wasn't as well oiled and orderly as they had always imagined.

*   *   *

I took a taxi straight to a small garage I know where a car can be borrowed with a minimum of fuss and three sets of licence plates. I drove around for a couple of hours until I was certain I wasn't being followed. Then I pointed the car west, and put my foot down.

It took me forty-five minutes to reach where I was going and the whole time I wasn't conscious of the road once. My thought processes were far too involved, sorting and classifying the permutations of what had been going on for the past few months. For the sake of accuracy, I cleared out all the garbage in my mind to start with and then, with a clean slate, I started to slot back the facts as I saw them. Whichever way I put the material in, it came out the same way.

It had started when I had read the report of Antonov's death. He'd had a preliminary heart attack and been moved from his cell to the prison hospital. Now prison hospitals may be fine for removing home-made shivs or mending bashed skulls, but intensive care units they definitely ain't. A man of Antonov's notoriety and importance would have been hot footed to the nearest large hospital where there was equipment and personnel to take care of coronary failures. Therefore it was logical to assume the heart attack had killed him right off. But, in that case, why the fiction of the two days lingering in the prison hospital? Unless he hadn't been in prison at all.

This was where my little man with the boils had come in. Fred Terry had dug me up a genuine, *bona fide* prison officer. Warmed by the fifty pounds I'd given him, he was adamant that not only had there not been a death in the prison hospital where he worked, heart attack or otherwise, but neither had there ever been a man named Antonov anywhere inside the walls. What he did recall very clearly was an occupied coffin arriving late one night with a minimum of fuss and a great deal of secrecy. The following morning the coffin had been collected and whipped off for burial to the accompaniment of sufficient publicity to spread the fact around.

'I must admit it 'ad me wonderin' at first,' he had said to me, scratching one of his boils with a dirty finger nail.

'Why only at first?' I'd asked.

He'd gone on to explain that once he'd read the official report in the newspapers, he'd stopped wondering because it was obviously being taken care of by Them.

'Who's Them?' I'd asked.

'Them,' he reiterated. 'You know – *Them. They.*'

It had taken me a couple of minutes to work out what the hell he was talking about. But then I'd got the drift. He'd gone on to say that who the hell ever knew what They were up to; They said all sorts of things whenever it suited Them; and it wasn't up to the likes of us to question what They were doing. As like as not They were doing it for our own good. I disagreed with him heartily on this point; not only did They do very little for anyone but Themselves; what They did do, They invariably cocked up. But They notwithstanding, Antonov had not died in prison, nor had he been anywhere near the place until he was long dead.

Once having digested this fact, it wasn't much of a problem to deduce that the announcement of his death had been delayed for a specific purpose. The timing was such that the purpose could only have had something to do with me. Antonov was dead before I went to Russia. Therefore I had been sent for a completely different purpose. I'd worked out a pretty fanciful theory as to what that purpose was, and tonight would see me right or dead.

*   *   *

If I was going to be dead, I'd chosen a pretty crummy place for it. Just outside Beaconsfield, there's a disused gravel pit that covers about forty acres. There was still gravel in it, but they'd dug so deep over the past twenty years that it had become uneconomic to continue. Five years earlier, they had realised it was costing them more to dig the stuff out and transport it than they could get for it. The company had gone broke and the receivers had stepped in. Faced with a lot of clapped out gravel shifting equipment, they did the most economic thing they could think of; they left it there to rot.

I pulled off the main road and bumped my way over half a mile of rutted track, trying to avoid the more obvious hazards. Finally I stopped the car and switched off the engine. The car gave a grateful grunt as it eased its tortured springs and.silence took over. I climbed out of the car and transferred my gun from raincoat pocket to the waist of my trousers. I made sure the safety catch was on – there was bumpy ground ahead and I didn't want to trip over and blow my own balls off. Leaving the car, I started to grope my way off to the left. There was a thin moon which spread sufficient diffused light to make the whole place lighter than a pitch black cellar, but not much. After two or three minutes and a badly bruised shin, my eyes adapted themselves sufficiently for me to check that I was heading in the right direction. Confirming this, the path I was on started to go downwards. I plodded on, the only person, as far as I could tell, for a couple of hundred miles in any direction.

I reached the bottom of the slope and pressed on. There was a quarter of a mile of flat, muddy ground, and then the path started upwards again. This one was steeper and by the time I reached the top, I was fit for bugger all. I was blowing like there was no tomorrow and my leg muscles were shaking like autumn leaves. It took me five minutes to recover. Finally I put myself back together again and got under way once more.

I'd chosen this particular place because when I had seen it in daylight it had seemed to provide everything I was looking for. If I had realised then the energy I was going to have to expend just to arrive at the meeting place, I would have settled for Hyde Park. What I couldn't see in the dark, but which I knew was there, was a huge, shallow basin, like a saucer, the side of which I had come down after leaving the car. On the far side of the saucer there was a wedge-shaped, flat-topped hillock, and this was what I was now traversing.

At the far side of this projection was the dilapidated wreckage of what had once been the gravel working equipment. There was a tall gravel washing tower, which had originally been fed by tipper trucks which reached it on a small gauge railway. I was reminded painfully of this as I tripped over one of the rails and landed with my knees on its companion. I dropped the torch I was carrying, and hadn't used yet, and spent three minutes feeling around trying to locate it. I was on the point of giving up all attempt at concealment and lighting a match, when I heard, very clearly and unmistakably, a foot shifting on gravel. For a few seconds after that all I could hear was my own heart thumping like a steam hammer from somewhere right between my ears. Then I managed to swallow hard and re-place my heart where it belonged before introducing myself.

'Leo?' I whispered. It came out like a dying croak. There was absolute silence for the space of five seconds. It seemed like five days. Then I heard the shifting of feet on gravel once more.

'Over here,' said Leo. He sounded damn near as frightened as I was. I climbed to my feet and, in doing so, I kicked the torch I had been groping for. I picked it up and, still not

switching it on, I tried to locate where 'over here' was. I
didn't need to; Leo suddenly loomed up beside me so silently
that he nearly had me going again. But I controlled an urgent
desire to scream out loud, and endeavoured to sound like the
master of the situation.

'You're early,' I said.

'So are you.'

'You've got the money?'

He nodded. 'I've got it. But first, what happens?'

'What should happen. You give me my half of the money
and we go our separate ways.'

'The information?'

'What information?'

'What you are selling.'

He must be barmy I thought. 'What good is it to you,' I
said. 'You're not going back to the CIA.'

'It still has a financial value,' he said. So that was it. He was
going to buy information with the CIA's money, then sell it
to someone else. It was pretty sneaky and he went up a notch
in my estimation. But it didn't really matter as from here on in
he wasn't going to do a thing that I hadn't already arranged for
him. I fished around through the slit in my raincoat pocket,
ostensibly searching for what I was supposed to be selling, but
in fact easing my gun from where it was tucked into the top of
my trousers. I didn't bother to release the safety catch as I
didn't expect I was going to have to use it. He, in turn, reached
into his inside pocket and produced a flat, bulky envelope that
could have held fifty thousand dollars. He handed me the envelope at the same time as I jabbed the gun into his stomach,
just about in line with where I had shot him seven years ago.
And he didn't bat an eyelid. In fact, as far as I could see in the

poor light, he seemed to relax slightly as though I had settled a point that had been worrying him. Keeping my gun tucked well into his middle, I groped around for the gun I knew he would be carrying, but which he wasn't. Feeling a mite safer I relaxed a little, but kept my gun where it was.

'Brought your suitcase?' I said.

'What's that supposed to imply?'

'You're going on a trip. Didn't you know?'

'I've made my own plans,' he said.

'I'll bet you have,' I said. 'But you may as well forget them. My plans are better.'

'Better for you, perhaps.'

'You'll survive,' I said, not believing it for a moment.

He was almost enjoying himself. 'And where will my survival take place?' he asked.

'Where else?' I said. 'Back home in Mother Russia.'

Through our connecting thirty-eight calibre umbilical, I thought I felt a stiffening of the muscles. Then he relaxed again.

'No, Mr Smith,' he said. 'It is not I who will be going anywhere; it is you.'

'Where?'

'Wherever Max decides to send you. To the grave I trust.'

'You don't want to take any notice of Max,' I said. 'He's a pathological liar. What did he tell you? That he'd send his cavalry in at at the last moment? Is that what he said?'

I'd obviously hit it right on the button because he stiffened up again. And to confirm the fact even more positively he glanced quickly over his shoulder. Although what he expected to see in the pitch dark, I had no idea.

'You're a pigeon, Leo,' I said. 'You're going to Russia.

Not because I made a deal with Borensko, but because the CIA and Max intend you to.'

I'd got through to him in spades now.

'I work for the CIA,' he said, as though it made a difference.

'Indeed you do,' I said. 'What delicious little titbits of information have you picked up during the past three years? You'd better start remembering because Borensko will want to know the lot.' He was silent for a moment, trying to take in what I was telling him. 'Think about it, Leo,' I said. 'Doesn't it strike you as odd that just because you decided three years ago that you wanted to change sides, the CIA fell over themselves to employ you. Why? You were mediocre at your job and they'd already got a full quota of mediocrities.'

'I gave them a great deal of useful information,' he finally managed.

'And no doubt they were grateful. As far as they were concerned it was a bonus. You were the man they wanted, not your information. For three years they've been filling you full of guff intending to deliver you back to Borensko at some later date for him to torture it out of you.'

'This can't be true.'

'I'm afraid it is. Did you know that Antonov was dead before I went to Russia?'

'No,'

'So why did they send me?' He didn't answer. So I filled him in, laying it out for myself at the same time. 'There had to be another reason, and you were it. They took a calculated risk that Borensko and I would come up with the idea ourselves. If we hadn't, I would have done my fifteen years and they'd have thought of something else.'

'But Max said . . .' He didn't finish.

'You went to Max after we met and made our little deal. You told him all about it and I'll bet I can quote you verbatim what he said. Meet Smith, pass over the money, and we've got him for working for the Russians. I'll have men standing by to pick him up. Right?' He didn't answer, but I was right never-the less. 'So forget it, Leo, you've been conned, same as me. There's no cavalry waiting to gallop to the rescue.'

'But they're here. I saw . . .' Before he could finish we heard the helicopter. It must have come in very low because it was only seconds after we first heard its chopping roar that it swooped past overhead. Still keeping the gun on Leo, I fished out my torch and switching it on, I waved it about a bit. A moment later the helicopter swung round, half a mile away, and started back towards us. At the same time a giant flood-light was switched on beneath the fuselage, bathing everything in glaring white light.

Then we were both ducking from the downdraft of the helicopter as it put down delicately, twenty-five feet from where we were standing.

'Come on,' I said, giving him a prod with the gun.

'No,' he said.

I jabbed him again. 'Yes,' I said. And all fight seemed to leak out of him. He started towards the helicopter with me follow-ing half a pace behind. As we drew near, the door in the side of the fuselage was opened and I could see a crewman standing, waiting. We reached the helicopter and Leo, an old man suddenly, started to climb in.

*   *   *

But during that short walk something he had just said suddenly cracked me on the back of the skull.

'They're here. I saw . . .'

He was right, of course. Leo *would* have seen them. He would have pointed out the meeting place and told them how he was going to play it. They may have been there just to keep Leo happy and play up the deception, but Max had always been a great one for killing two birds with one stone. I suddenly knew who the second bird was going to be. I jabbed Leo with the gun as the crewman reached down to help him in.

'Not this trip, Leo,' I said. He turned and looked at me, not understanding. 'I'm going instead,' I said.

I stepped past him and climbed into the helicopter. I nodded to the crewman as he closed the door and he signalled forward to the pilot. The helicopter shook beneath us and started to rise almost immediately. I turned to the window, looking down at the diminishing figure of Leo, who was staring up at us, oblivious to the enormous downdraft.

'Switch off the light,' I yelled to the crewman, hoping Borensko would have had the sense to send someone who could speak English. The man pressed a switch and for a moment Leo was lost in the blackness below. Then suddenly another light flashed on. It was a spotlight located somewhere on the other side of the gravel pit. It hovered, searching for a second, then it fixed on Leo. He turned towards it and I think he realised what was going to happen a split second before he died, because he put his hands up, waving them wildly, and started to run in the direction of the light. There were half a dozen stabs of flame from behind the spotlight. I thought I heard the sound of the shots over the noise of the helicopter, but it was probably imagination. The figure of Leo was arrested in mid-flight, as though he had run straight into an invisible wall. Then he was knocked backwards off his feet.

The last I saw of him, as the helicopter swung round and made off fast, was a lifeless rag doll figure, sprawled out in the beam of the floodlight. Then that, too, was extinguished leaving nothing but blackness.

I walked up front to the pilot's cabin and tapped him on the shoulder. The crewman was close behind me, not having any idea what was going on. He was nervous and he fingered the holstered gun at his belt as though there was a possibility he might have to use it. I shouted to the pilot.

'You've got about five minutes before Max realises he's had the wrong man killed.'

The pilot grinned up at me and, taking that as a sign that five minutes was all he needed, I moved back into the passenger cabin. I sat down and a moment later the crewman, who must have been watching my face, handed me a plastic bag. I didn't even have time to thank him before I was noisily sick.

*   *   *

It was Leningrad this time. Men like Borensko didn't often travel outside Moscow, but it seemed there was a minor purge on in Leningrad and he was here to see that there wasn't any fair play.

When he recovered from his initial nastiness, he was affability itself. He'd been expecting a valuable Leo Tamir; what he got was an apparently worthless John Smith. But when he'd settled down a bit and put away the thumbscrews, I managed to explain how well off he was.

'The whole thing was designed to get Leo Tamir back here,' I said. 'For three years he's been working for the CIA and they've been feeding him false information. All he knew was

186

what the CIA intended you to find out, and you can guess how useful *that* would have been.'

Borensko poured me another drink, even getting to his feet to do so.

'Max knew I was going to push Leo into the helicopter. That was the whole idea. Then, to make sure I didn't get loud-mouthed afterwards, he had his Heavy Squad waiting to gun me down the moment Leo left. That's why I got on the 'copter and left Leo. They thought it was me. Bang, bang! Good-bye, Leo. And good-bye grand design.'

He refilled my glass.

'What do we do with you now, Mr Smith?' he asked.

'You give me Anne Ballard, your blessing, and two first class aeroplane tickets to London.'

'We don't have first class on our aeroplanes. Ours is a classless society.'

I grinned at him to show that I didn't believe it either.

'What is to stop me from sending you back to prison?'

'You wouldn't do that,' I said. 'There'd be no point.'

He knew I was right. I'd been framed into the whole deal from the off, and it was going to do no one any good at all to lock me up for fifteen years. Also, in the back of his mind, there was no doubt lurking the nasty idea that perhaps, some-where in the future, he'd be able to use me now that contact had been established. I didn't disillusion him.

'What are you going to do?' he asked.

'Pick up Anne Ballard and go back to London.'

'Is that safe? Max will be very angry.'

'He'll be even angrier when I ask for the seven and a half thousand pounds he still owes me.'

'He won't pay.'

'He'll have to. Because if he doesn't I'll tell the CIA that it was his men who killed Leo. The CIA have worked very hard for three years on this little scheme. They're going to be choked that it's gone up in smoke. Max will have spun them some yarn to cover up his cock-up. But you can bet your life it won't be the true one. Only I can do that. And that's why he'll pay me.'

The conversation drifted on after that. Borensko asked a few more questions and I answered them as best I could. Then he grew bored with the whole thing.

'You are fortunate, Mr Smith,' he said getting to his feet. 'Miss Ballard's theatrical group are performing in Leningrad this week. I'll have you driven to the theatre.'

At the door he shook my hand warmly, and I almost liked him for a moment, revolving eye notwithstanding.

'You and Miss Ballard,' he said, just before he let me go. 'You have something between you?'

'I'm working on it,' I said. He looked curious for one moment.

'You've not . . . I mean to say, have you yet . . .?'

'No,' I said. 'But we've our whole lives in front of us.'

He laughed then, the first genuine laughter I had heard from him. He threw back his head and he roared. I thought his bad eye was going to revolve its way clean out of its socket. I stood there politely, with an inane grin on my face, wondering if he was going to enlighten me. But he didn't. Finally he pulled himself together.

'Good-bye, John Smith,' he said. Then he handed me over to his driver.

The driver had been given his instructions and, while I sat in the back of the car sharpening up my hormones, he drove me to the theatre. There, he had a word with the stage door keeper, and I was passed through backstage.

I saw Anne almost immediately. She was standing in the wings, waiting to go on. She was with one of the acrobats I had seen perform in Moscow. They were holding hands and, as I watched, they turned to each other, smiled a secret sort of smile reserved for lovers, and they kissed. It was the sort of kiss that left no doubt as to their relationship.

I backed out of the theatre quietly and had the car take me straight to the airport.

Borensko had been wrong; there was a first class section on the aeroplane. But it was full up, and I sat with the peasants.

I put Anglo Soviet relations back ten years during that journey. I shouted at the stewardess; I complained to the captain who was ill-advised enough to ask me how I was enjoying the flight; I sent back the caviare; I insulted three other passengers; and if I'd had a razor I would probably have slashed the seats.

*   *   *

No wonder Borensko had laughed. No doubt in ten or twelve years I'd see the funny side of it myself. After all, I had been through a great deal for that bird and now here she was, in love with someone else. I don't think I'd have minded as much as I did if she'd chosen one of the other acrobats in the group. But out of the two fellows and the girl, Anne had chosen the girl.

THE END